WITHDRAWN

DEAR READER

There's a pile of books that have to be read, that every-body's read, that I've not read, probably because I thought that they'd been read sufficiently without needing me to read them as well; meanwhile I read other books.

—FRANÇOIS CARADEC

"No one knows what makes books sell."
"I've heard that before," Garp said.

—JOHN IRVING,
The World According to Garp

PAUL FOURNEL
DEAR READER

Translated from the French by
David Bellos

PUSHKIN PRESS
LONDON

Pushkin Press
71–75 Shelton Street, London WC2H 9JQ

Original text © P.O.L. 2012

English translation © David Bellos 2014

Originally published in French as *La liseuse* in 2012

This translation first published by Pushkin Press in 2014

0 0 2

ISBN 978 1 782270 26 3

Title pages and frontispiece frame by Jean Jullien

Set in 10 on 13.5 Monotype Baskerville by Tetragon, London

Proudly printed and bound in Great Britain by TJ International,
Padstow, Cornwall on Munken Premium White 90gsm

www.pushkinpress.com

I

For a long time I would put my feet on it for a spot of rest and elevation and so as to improve circulation to the brain, but nowadays I find with increasing frequency that I lay my head on it, particularly in the evening, Friday evenings especially. I fold my arms around the manuscript, rest my forehead on the crook of my arm and my cheek on the virgin paper. The wood my desk is made of amplifies the sound of my heart. Well-aged art deco furniture makes an excellent conductor of feelings and fatigue. Is it a Ruhlmann? Or a piece from Leleu? My good old desk has seen it all. I listen to my heart, my Friday heart, my old heart beating in the silent house. At this hour everyone else has gone home and I'm the last man on deck, all alone on a losing streak because I haven't had the heart to pile up the towering monument of manuscripts I have to take home for the weekend. Same as every Friday.

The one under my cheek has a love theme: it's about a guy who meets a girl but he's got a wife and she's got a boyfriend… I've read seven pages and I know the rest already. Nothing's going to give me a surprise any more. For years I've not really read anything, because all I do is reread. I spend my time rereading the same brew that gets served up

9

as literary sensations, lead titles, seasonal launches, runaway successes, flops and more flops. Paper for pulping, in trucks that set off at dawn and return at dusk full to the gunwales of obsolete new books.

When was it exactly that I stopped jumping for joy at the mere thought that I might discover a masterpiece and come back into the office on a Monday morning a new man? Twenty years ago? Could it be thirty? I don't like doing sums of that sort, they have a whiff of mortality about them. When I close my eyes the steady yellow glow of the Perzel lamp passes through my eyelids and summons up black whorls and floating ruins like a drawing by Victor Hugo. My breathing slows down as does my cardiac rhythm somewhat. I could easily drop off. I could die. Yes! Like Molière, I could die in the saddle. They'd say, "He died as he lived, among books, whilst reading!" and to be honest I would have passed on while dreaming of nothing. I haven't really read properly for a long time. Do I still know how to read—I mean, to read in the full sense of the word? Am I still up to it? If I let my head loll to the side, my heart beats louder and sends a shiver through the oak...

The whole house is bathed in the silence of old paper. Books, like snow, gobble up sound. My profession has its own smell and mufflers. I can smell it better in this quiet. Going back into the noise of the world is always a challenge.

Who's that knocking at my door? I don't recognize that gentle, brief and polite taptaptap. The knuckle must be very small.

"Come in!"

She enters. I've never seen her before. A pang of nostalgia grips me, nostalgia for the good old days when the firm was small enough for me to know every girl in the office by the shape of her calves. This one has a nice face. Her wide-eyed stare suggests that mine is somewhat the worse for wear. Probably red pressure lines on my cheek from leaning it on my jacket sleeve.

"Am I interrupting?"

"Not fatally, young lady. Who are you?"

"Er, I'm the intern."

"Which department?"

"I wasn't told. You know, interns get lumbered with so much stuff, they have to be adaptable."

"Do you want a raise?"

"No, I'm unpaid."

She seems fairly startled, her jeans are torn and the rest of her chromatic. She's short, has black eyes, looks nice, but I'd have a hard time telling if she's pretty. I can't read these kinds of girls either any more. She's lively. Is she from Normale Sup'? Or from the College of Printing—the mill that churns out a thousand Gaston Gallimards a year, the better to pulp them later on?

"No. Arts Administration."

"Really? You want to minister to publishing? I wish you the very best of luck."

"I'd rather run concerts."

"Sit down."

"I can't stay. It's Friday. It's late."

"Five minutes. You want to run concerts?"

"Yeah, music is great."

"So what are you doing here?"

"I like books as well! Anyway, there was an opening. We have to do a placement. Compulsory."

"And if I may be so bold as to inquire, what are you doing in my office?"

"The big boss, Monsieur Meunier, told me to…"

"Is that what he's called? Meunier?"

"Don't you know him?"

"Only too well."

"So you know. He told me to bring you this."

"*This* being what, precisely?"

"Er, it's a reader. A Kandle. An iClone. One of those gizmos. He said he'd put all your weekend manuscripts on it, it would take a weight off your shoulder. Do you want me to show you? Look, it's like a screen with all your manuscripts on it. They're on your genuine wood-style virtual bookshelf. One tap and they open. There's a heap of them. You're never going to get through all that in two days! Look, this is how you open a book."

"How do I go to the next page?"

"You turn pages by sliding the corner on the bottom."

"Like a book?"

"Yep, that's the prehistoric side of it. A sop for seniors. When people have forgotten about books they'll wonder

why it works that way. Vertical makes more sense. Scrolling down would be more logical."

"Jack Kerouac will be pleased."

She doesn't get it.

"OK, I'm sorry, sir, I have to rush, I have a plane to catch. Don't read too much!"

"At my age…"

She disappears in a jiggle of buttock, closes the door gently behind her, and leaves me stroking my reader. It's black, cold, hostile and does not like me. There's no protruding button, no handle to hold it by or to swing it around like a slender briefcase, it's just hi-tech bling as classy as a Swedish brunette. Matte black or pitch dark (take your pick), smooth, soft, mirror-faced, and not heavy at all. I weigh it in my hand.

I put it on my desk and put my cheek on it. It's cold, silent, doesn't crumple or stain. There's no sign that it's got all those books in its belly. But it's really inconvenient. It's small enough to swim around in my briefcase, but too big to slip in my pocket.

In fact it has a lot in common with Meunier, the big boss. Not well suited to the task.

What was it the kid intern just said about books and concerts? In a way I'm going to have to let my briefcase go too, it's become too big for the job. I've schlepped it around since I was in my last year at school, and parting is going to be hard on us both. We were really very fond of each other, even if we never said it out loud. When it was properly packed

on a Friday night it felt just the right weight for work. It's the reason why my left shoulder is slightly lower than the right. Workplace disability. Quasimodo.

What I'll need now is a slipcase for my little reader. With a handle, if you please. I'm sure Meunier already has one in his desk drawer and that he'll turn up with it in triumph on Monday morning, when he comes to gather my opinion of his great discovery. "You have to keep up with the times, Gaston!" He's always liked calling me Gaston. Perhaps he thinks I like it too. Unless he thinks it's a joke. I'm not a fool and I know his gift won't be from Hermès or even Longchamp. I guess it will be some kind of mock croc with a foam lining to absorb knocks and bumps. Like the man himself.

I'm on my way, I have to be on my way. But let me stay behind another minute to lie on my desk—just for a minute—with my nose in a manuscript, so as to smell it one last time. For the truth about publishing is that the sensation in your nostrils can tell you as much about a book as an hour of close reading.

2

I cannot stand the countryside. That's why I go there every weekend. So as to read and have a heart attack in enemy territory, in dark and lugubrious silence. As I gave up having a good night's sleep long ago, I get out of bed in the pitch dark of the back of beyond and automatically dive into the thickest of my weekend doorstops. I sink onto the sofa, wrap my legs in a blanket, and read. My habitual technique is quite simple: I stack the pile of sheets on my paunch, and as I read I transfer them one by one to my chest. The increasing pressure on my ribcage gives an accurate reading of how much work I have done. For the first twenty pages I read with great attention, as slowly as I can make myself read, then I speed up gently, allowing my professional experience and what I know of the author and the book's concept to take over—imagination does the rest. This is my semi-somnolent reading style, which constitutes my deepest mode of engagement with a text. It's the perfect time for working on authors that the firm has published for many years—solid old troopers who need nothing more than a tuck or a nip.

The tablet is on my paunch. I hold it in both hands. There is a page open on the screen. I've matched the font size to the

strength of my half-moons. The reader is cold to the touch. It'll take a minute for my hands to warm it up. My reading lamp makes an unpleasant glare in one corner of the screen. I switch it off. Now the only light comes from the text. That's a plus. If I look at myself in the mirror, with the tablet under my chin, I look like a ghost. I am the ghost of readers past.

With a flick of a finger I turn pages that don't fall on any pile. They depart body and soul to some imaginary place I can hardly imagine. My chest is anxious and gives me no guide to how far I've got. There's no noise of turning pages to break the silence of the house. I miss the slight breeze I used to feel on my neck from each page as it fell. I am hot. The light from the page absorbs my eyes. I've suddenly lost a character and I have to go back. My useless pencil is still behind my ear (I'm a bookie reader) and I'm puzzled as to how I'm going to keep track of typos. I'm really put off by the idea of summoning up a keyboard the way the intern showed me and barging into the text. I've always been a man of margins and lead pencils. I want to be erasable. For a second I rest the reader on my chest and close my eyes. I'm waiting for the screen to go to sleep so I can too, just for fifteen minutes, until dawn comes.

The second reading session of my ritual day is located in the café. As soon as it opens. The first ferrous double shot of the day is mine. An unchanging espresso hand-pumped by the unchanging Albert, whom I've known since our schooldays, a man of few words and striking habits.

*

"Are you schlepping a TV around with you these days?"

"As you can see."

"No more reams?"

"I'm into crease-proof."

"Here's your poison. As soon as Marco opens up, I'll fetch your croissant."

As the café noise begins to increase bit by bit, it's time for the kind of reading that bucks me up. The early birds come in for their doses of coffee-with-calvados or white wine spritzers. A slow start to the day. Saturday is long. This is when I read detective novels. The radio on a shelf behind the bar produces a background track mixing murders in and out of the sentences I'm reading. A merging of murders. I can usually distinguish which ones belong to the manuscript because I know how they end, but the others float off in a fog of endless beginnings. Albert leaves me alone and so do the others, because I'm part of the furniture and don't make a noise. I keep it up until the card players arrive. Then the spasmodic sounds of new hands, ritual squabbles, and cards being called force me outside.

I've made a greasy stain on the screen. It must be from Marco's croissant. Albert lends me his wet bar-rag to wipe it clean. I give it a dry finish with my sleeve and go out. I wonder whether the tablet is waterproof.

It's the ideal time to go to my bench in the park. It's not sunny. It's not raining. It's time for reading poems under the lime. I can't manage to find them in this darned black box. I hunt all over the place to find my poems. It would be just

like Meunier to hide them away. To warn me not to persist in the fantastical idea of bringing them out. "Another black hole, Gaston! Poetry is a bottomless pit!"

If the poems are any good, they make this the nicest part of the day. The temperature is on the rise, the kids are shouting off scale, I fold one leg under the other on the bench and I sing the poems to myself. Progress slows to a pitiable speed as I dawdle, go back on my tracks, hesitate, recite, and waste precious time. Vacation time, so to speak. I rest my dear reader in my lap, I look around. Soon I'm thinking of other poems, and then others beside. In a trice I'm thinking about nothing at all. I'm backing off.

Sometimes Adèle comes to join me. Over the years she's learned exactly what time my mind begins to wander so she can slip in and winch me back home to normality. To the normality of people who read no more than one hour a day, the normality of the monumental Middle-aged Mother of Two, at whose oracular feet all publishers lay down their lists, their retail distribution arrangements and their promotional campaigns. Adèle usually comes from the other end of the park. When I see that head of white hair and the rubbery stride that's no longer as bouncy as it was, I know it is time.

Today she's not coming. She told me she wanted to sleep in, and as a result I'm lumbered with the shopping. I've not forgotten about it, but it means I'll have to snap out of my daze all by myself. She even added that she'd wait until siesta time to filch my reader from me. She has clever fingers and a

quick mind. Whereas I'm a slowcoach and stick to the tricks I know. A reader, yes, but an explorer, no.

"Say, René, would you mind weighing this for me?"

The butcher, an upright man in a bloody apron with his cleavers set criss-cross in pockets on his paunch, takes my reader without demur and puts it on the scales. The needle wobbles for a second.

"730 grams without the rind, Robert, my friend!"

"Or a bit over?"

"As always. Can I have a look at your toy? How do you switch it on?"

"Press on the dimple at the bottom."

So that's the final weight of world literature as it sits in René's fat red fingers. 730 grams. Cervantes, Hugo, Dickens, and Proust make just 730 grams. Want to throw in Perec? 730 grams. Rilke as well? Just 730 grams.

"I'll have two rump steaks, René."

"Up and coming! Specially for you. Here, take your gizmo back. I put some blood on it. The kids are going to be after it. Can you watch TV on it?"

René slices two steaks with his forefingers folded on the side of the blade, a nice trick he learned from his father. He lays them on grease-proof paper as if they were old masters. Butchering doesn't change. The knives are the same, the

meat is the same. There's no butchers' revolution marching ever on.

"You see, René, you've got the joint on one side of you and the grease-proof paper on the other. Well, that's how it is for me too. Text on one side and paper on the other. From now on they're not permanently stuck together."

I'm going to ask Marco the pastry chef to weigh my reader a second time, to confirm the true weight of world literature and the final demise of the doorstop. With a bit of luck, he'll anoint it with a dollop of cream.

3

"What's that sticking plaster on your nose? Did you get into a fight?"

"I fell asleep reading, and my dear reader toppled onto me. All seven hundred and thirty certified grams of it. Something like that really wakes you up. Another siesta ruined. My nose can take it. But I do have to admit that I keep squinting at the dressing... What's on the menu for today?"

I like Sabine a lot. She's a redhead. It would be a good idea for every firm to have a redhead on its staff. I like going into her office, which is next to mine. When I come in, she swings round on her chair to face me, as if we were going to have a fight. Actually, we have a game: I pretend not to know what's on my plate, and she pretends to be in complete control of my schedule. She knows everything about me, and I know a fair bit about her too. On closer inspection, she runs the firm and loves to prove it. She used to be incredibly good-looking and now at thirty-something she is creditably handsome. How many writers stayed with us because of her? How many passionate affairs has she had? She has come through upheavals and lay-offs. On the day I hired her, maybe ten years ago, I remember thinking: "A character like that won't

last ten days, but I have to have someone." That's how much insight I have into the female of the species.

"The guys in production want to see you at 1:15, and then you've got Balmer for lunch."

"Which eatery?"

"I made a reservation at the Tilbury. Is that OK?"

"As always. What does Balmer want?"

"Nothing. It's just time to give him a kick in the pants. He got a big advance and Meunier's worried about him taking it easy."

"Meunier doesn't know a pro from a purse. Balmer has always met his deadlines."

"Many a time and oft…"

"Was that supposed to be a pun? Did you send the email to the Yanks?"

"Yes, boss."

Mme Martin, the owner of the Tilbury, is exactly as old as Pauline Réage. In addition she can be held responsible for the waist measurements of most of my colleagues in French publishing. She serves heavy, slow-cooked food, like an ethnic granny in exile in the Valley of Books. It was because of her, I recall, that I nearly dropped the idea of launching my own company when I was a young man: the sight of my protuberant elders waddling ponderously around the publishing district gave me a real fright. I really had no wish to end up like them. Fortunately there

were two notorious ascetics who balanced things out by performing lunch assignments with just a bottle of spring water. They were the Stone Commanders of the profession. Giacomettis. I took the plunge. When all's said and done I haven't made any money out of publishing but I have eaten rather well.

"I've put you at your usual table, M Dubois."

"That's sweet of you, Mme Martin."

Allocating a round table to only two diners is an act of kindness in an area where floor space has a price beyond rubies.

"With all the times you've been here and all you've managed to eat, you must own half the restaurant by now!"

"I've no objection!"

"I've made a blanquette today."

"I'll wait for Balmer, but give me something to drink meanwhile."

"Bouzy as usual?"

"You said it!"

It's a wonder to see her doing her two-step round the tables. Week in, week out she picks up scraps of conversation and knows all the inside stories. For instance, I'd really like her to tell me what the fat man in the back is cooking up, such as which of my writers he's going to promise bright lights and rich pickings and lure away this year…

"Here's your bouzy to keep you going. Cold enough? I've got a decent bordeaux as well…"

"No way. You see, I rise early and I'm always first in the office. I work like a Trojan. I get through the straightforward, crucial stuff before lunch. Do you remember, twenty years ago we used to lunch at 12:30? Then it slipped to 1, and now it's 1:30. The lag leaves me with lots of time. So at lunch I can now drink with gay abandon and have woozy afternoons. It allows me to take fuzzy and occasionally strange decisions. They're really necessary, because publishing is a rational business, on the one hand, but on the other it is also random. Even crazy, and there's no harm if it's a little boozy. That's how I do the job, anyway. The people down the line who decant our products into Handbooks and Companions not to mention Bluffers' Guides cash in very nicely. They can afford top-of-the-range bordeaux! Excuse me… Hallo, yes? Is that you? Balmer, do you want me to die of starvation? It's past half past…"

"Don't wait for me, this is too much. I'm at Softbook and I'm running late. They want me to write things for Kandles and iClones. It's a gas! I can cast away the rusty chains that lock print and paper to big prizes. You can do loads of entertaining ficlets. You should take a look. There's a continent to explore…"

"Now don't you forget you owe me an absolutely conventional thing called a book. Of the right old kind."

"No, I've not forgotten, but believe me, this is going to be tremendous. You should be in on it. They're brilliant. Must go. I'll tell you all about it…"

A technological revolution is surely the only thing that

could ever make me lunch solo. It never happens, but if it does perchance occur, I wouldn't think of a sit-down restaurant. A sandwich and a glass of bouzy at the Croix-Rouge café is more than enough for me.

"I'm doubly sorry about the lovely table you've given me, Mme Martin. I find I'm obliged to lunch on my own."

"Well, that's an innovation, M Dubois. What would you like?"

"I'd like artichoke for starters."

"Warm?"

"Yes. And lamb's brains *meunière* for mains."

The artichoke is a dish for the lonesome, because it is difficult to eat when facing someone else and quite divine when you're on your own. It is a contemplative legume, perfectly suited to dexterous foodies. First come the hard fleshy parts; then, leaf by leaf, comes softer and subtler stuff. Green slowly shades into grey and then the last little cap of purple comes right off to reveal the beige tuft. As the texture changes so the sauce reinvigorates the taste. You take the trip at your own speed. There's no need to hurry an artichoke. You can suck a single leaf for minutes on end until it turns sour, or, on the contrary, you can snatch several leaves in a bunch and scour them with your front teeth to extract a solid mouthful. The only procedure that's out of bounds is guzzling. Artichokes require a degree of elegance. At long last you reach the entertaining removal of the tuft. You take the hair between

your thumb and the side of your knife and, if pulled gently, it comes off in small, neat quiffs to reveal the heart in all its glory, in a startling and very brief simulation of sex. Now the reward: use your knife and fork to enter the veggie heart directly, praying that the grower has left it free of the slightest trace of pastiness.

At that very moment Mme Martin discreetly steers a small dish towards me with an extra helping of sauce, toned down with a dash of crème fraiche.

Does the artichoke have a place in literature? Is there a book, a page or a paragraph truly worthy of it? I must check this evening.

Sit back in seat, clean palate with bread before taking a mouthful of bouzy (it doesn't go with vinaigrette) and wait for the heavenly brain, to be dissected so easily with just a fork and then left to melt between tongue and roof of mouth. Another dish for the single diner. Intellectuals hate seeing people eat their brains. Ordering brains at lunch is in really poor taste, especially when done by a publisher.

4

"Am I right, Gaston? Isn't it brilliant? Don't tell me my tablet isn't magic!"

"I noticed it has a tendency to hide poems."

"Spoilsport! You've got two left thumbs, and you're too lazy to explore."

"Then I wanted to read on the train back to town, but it was out of juice. In those circumstances it's a waste of space."

"You should think ahead!"

"Lastly, it's done my nose in. I plan on taking disability leave for a few weeks and counting the event as a workplace injury. Our health and safety procedures will need revising."

"It won't happen again. Look, I've brought you a padded case. It's black and very smart. It weighs nothing, and it's made out of a plastic that looks just like croc…"

Meunier. No need for tea-leaves to work out what he'll do next. The first time he came into my office what I saw was a baby in grown-up clothing. He had a fat puffy face on top of a tie that was ugly though dark, a shirt that was second-rate though white, and a suit that was ill cut though grey. He was fresh out of his MBA, and had turned up to do an audit on me. He'd been sent in by the suits running the

conglomerate that had just bought me out, to shed light on what were already transparent accounts—so transparent, in fact, that you could see through to the other side. My jangled nerves had barely recovered from four mass-market launches that fizzled and two best-selling beach books that weren't. Cash-flow was all in the wrong direction. Oddly enough, I felt like putting my boot in his backside, but beneath his outward shell of idiocy I thought he was quite smart. I recall that I even resolved to give him an education and make him understand, so he would stop poring over the books.

After a whole week of working every night until ten, he marched triumphantly into my office and announced:

"I've found the solution to your problem, M Dubois!"

He shuffled a sheaf of paperwork and explained:

"All you have to do is pull all the books that sell less than 15,000 copies, and then you'll be above water. And if you let two employees go, you could even get into the black inside a year."

Oddly enough (I've never stopped being surprised by Meunier, which only goes to show how much insight I have into the male of the species), I did not slap his face. After a lengthy pause I opened my right-hand drawer and took out that year's list.

"Very clever, Mistah Meunier. Here's this year's list. Please use a finger to point to all the books that will sell less than 15,000 copies. I will be only too pleased to strike them down."

*

He looked through the list in all seriousness, like a good boy at school, then gave up.

"That's difficult," he conceded, "I don't know all the names."

"Usually, this is how it goes. Even when you know the names, you only know *afterwards* whether or not their books have sold 15,000 copies. What you need to know about are the buyers."

"You just have to do market research ahead of time."

"Mistah Meunier, do you know how much market surveys cost? Don't answer. Three times what a book is worth. People have got into the awkward habit of putting out books just to see how many copies they sell. It's called publishing. Incidentally, that is what I do."

Over the following days I saw him wandering around the building with his necktie loose, then in his pocket, with his synapses firing non-stop as he tried to put the pieces together again. But I'd put the worm in the apple. After that there was Geneviève and the all-night love-in, and that was the end of him. She's a giraffe who does nothing but write during the day and gobble up young men after dinner to rejuvenate her brain. She told him all about the agonies and the ecstasies of the writer's craft and twisted him round her little finger. In the next few weeks he discovered an astronomical number of new writers, and he was bitten. Publishing can be sexually transmitted—on which more anon. But he's been breathing down my neck since then. He turned down a prince's ransom

from McKindle and, with the blessing of the Big Money that showers its peanuts on me, he's decided to pretend to be a publisher. He gets on my nerves.

Now and again when Meunier irritates me beyond endurance I ask Geneviève to disconnect him. She does it solely for my sake, because she prefers alternation. She sequesters the man for a few days, traps him between her long legs and recalibrates him in a book-friendly direction, and then forces him to put up with two or three silent writing sessions. She sits in her bedroom at her computer writing a love story, and he's not allowed to waggle his head or his tail until she's quite finished.

"Look here, you idiot," she says to him. "It's easy to say no to a writer in two ticks, it's easy to poke fun at what he does. What you have to learn is that writing books is a long and dreary task. Even bad ones. Especially bad ones."

So back he comes to the office in a better, more relaxed, more adaptable and more publishing-friendly state. Geneviève is pure magic. That is why I will never turn down anything she sends in and will always get her ad in *Elle* to launch each new book she writes. She loves seeing her own photo in women's magazines. It's been a while since she's been to see me, though. I'm going to have to take her out to the Tilbury.

"I've read the manuscript Boudon passed on to us. It's about a guy who meets a girl. The guy is married and the girl has

a boyfriend… The story's OK, but I really can't imagine what made Boudon give it to us. It's nothing but pouting lips, pencil brows, sun-kissed skin… That sort of prose."

Meunier is still a new boy. He loves tearing strips off writers. Each to his own way of wasting time. As there's no shortage of manuscripts to rubbish, you might as well save your breath.

"One good thing about digital publishing is that you can take risks with books of that sort. Loads of new readers will come flocking."

"Well, if I knew how to do it, I'd rather watch movies on a tablet. After all, it looks much more like a television than a book. A nice little serial to watch while you're eating in the canteen, or on the bus, or in the loo. *The Contraltos*, *The Wretched of Saint-Germain-des-Prés*, something like that. You can even watch them in Esperanto with Chinese sub-titles…"

Sabine enters my office redheadedly.

"Boss, get Meunier off my back, we've got real work to do! Come on, get him out! The man's a real pest. Not only does that parasite do nothing all day long, but he also stops you from working. This morning I caught him in his office, in front of the mirror, combing his eyebrows! Last night he scolded the interns for going home at seven! That really takes the biscuit, because the kids aren't even paid. One day I'll make him weep."

"Meanwhile, what is to be done?"

"I've got the numbers. Not good."

"Worse than usual?"

"Look at the returns. It's a tidal wave. If we send out ten truckloads of books to irrigate the nation in the morning, we get six of them back in the evening. What's the point?"

"A significant part of the publishing industry consists of burning diesel. You've been in it long enough to know that…"

"It's getting worse and worse. Don't tell me that books get a chance when they're displayed on bookshop tables. The booksellers slip them under the counter, then send them straight back. Don't pretend you're not looking at the figures, it's really annoying. Would you like a piece of dark chocolate?"

"We took everything out of books that used to be in them to sell more copies, and now we're not selling any. It's our own mistake."

5

"Come on in! I know you're my evening intern from the way you knock on the door like the ghost of a mouse. Sit down."

"I just wanted to find out how you got on with the reader over the weekend. Did you manage?"

"I coped with it just fine until I forgot to put it on recharge. That's when it got complicated. I tried shaking the thing and blowing on it. I even tried a head-butt—you can see my scars. Nothing doing. It stayed dark. I have to admit, when the reader's in that state, it's very relaxing."

"It's quite true that books don't have to be put on recharge. Whatever you may think, I like books, actually. Yes I do—even me. I always have one in my coat pocket, but I have to abandon it on an empty seat in the Métro because there's no room in my room."

"What's your name? A thought of that calibre ought to have an author credit."

"The name's Valentine. Valentine Tijean. What about you, if you don't mind my asking?"

"I usually answer to the name of Robert Dubois."

"Robert Dubois! Same name as the publishing house!

'Robert Dubois Books'! It must be strange to have the same name as the firm."

"You get used to it."

"M Meunier must be tickled pink."

"What seems to tickle him is calling me Gaston."

"Why Gaston?"

"I can't begin to explain."

She's sitting on the Chesterfield in my office. Her left knee is bare which enables me to observe that she's no longer got any scabs or sticking plasters on it. It can't be very long since. She is shod in flower-patterned Doc Martens. She's right up to the mark of last year's fashion. I like her. She knows nothing, she wants everything, she is the future of my profession.

"Tell me, you must be in the know. Where do they put all these darned interns we have in the firm? Apparently there's a whole year-group but I never see any of them. Apart from you, of course."

"There're always six or seven of us, but it's a floating population. Most of us are from Normale Sup' and Sciences Po. There are never any quants, and wannabe tycoons try to get placed with the majors, in case they can pick up some dosh."

"There's not much risk you'll find any of that around here, for sure."

"I know, but publishing is fun. You can read new books and you get to meet authors when they come in to sign copies."

"They're not as much fun as singers, wouldn't you say?"

"I'm keener on guitarists, actually. Star strummers. But still I'd like to meet Jean-Marie Le Clézio."

"Do you think you could set up a little meeting with your fellow-interns after work one day? Just you lot and me, here in my office."

"No problem."

"Thanks. Let's do it quite late, in the evening. In the meantime… grab this typescript, one of the prehistoric kind, on 80-gram paper. Read it and tell me what you think of it."

"But I'm not a reader…"

"Something tells me nonetheless that you have learned the alphabet. You never know."

I save time in the evenings since I've stopped looking in local shop windows since they've stopped having any books in them and slim-line jackets and pointy-toed shoes have ceased to be my size. I save more time by not having a drink with colleagues before going home as all we have to say to each other in any case is that we're publishing too many useless books and we have to stop, but everyone's doing ten per cent more each year than the last. I save yet more time by not dining in town because I've lost my appetite for dinners of that kind.

Despite its padded case my tablet swims about in my briefcase and I can feel it knocking against my thigh. It's a briefcase I can't easily part with because it's got a dog-eared paperback inside it (Maurice Pons, *Les Saisons*, as a penance

35

for having failed to pick it up), as well as a blank book like the ones I gave my writers for Christmas ten years ago, a Sheaffer fountain pen and my Victorinox pen-knife with corkscrew. I never use it but I always tell myself I might use it. Maybe when the world as we know it comes to an end? When we all go together when we go? Or maybe I'll use it surreptitiously when they won't allow me to have a knife at table any more because I'm too far gone? Sometime soon people will perhaps also have surreptitious books the way I have my secret knife. Useless, but a great comfort. With a corkscrew. Home is 788 paces from the office this evening.

Adèle likes my tablet. She impounds it while I'm slicing potatoes for a gratin; I'll add some cream and some mushrooms, which will do in lieu of meat. Adèle has located the games. I can hear little pfft pfft noises each time she knocks out a head in mah-jong. For the length of the meal she dutifully puts it on recharge. She tells me she's had enough of journalists. Adèle has always told me she's had enough of journalists. She must have fallen out of love with her job. I was quite prepared to take any job in publishing, myself—except publicity. That's why I married her. Together we constitute a fully formed publishing house. Not the same house, that's only sensible, but fully formed all the same. This evening we're drinking vacqueyras just to be jolly.

During the night I can hear the modest rumble of the street. In the darkened house I can imagine the gleam of the street-lamps. Adèle keeps coughing in her sleep. Maybe she's dreaming of Bernard Pivot? The tablet is on my lap and I'm

reading the story of a guy who meets a girl and I suddenly feel I need to look up a word in the dictionary. That's also been hidden in the belly of the machine. A Nano-Collins. As I track it down I stumble on the television app. It's a real television, same size as a book I could be holding in my hand. I watch it in the dark with my face lit up by Juliette Binoche's. She's on the brink of being raped by a werewolf. How could I leave her in such a dire predicament? What if I stopped reading for good?

It's her fault that I'm sleepy and over-committed in the morning because I spent the night doing nothing at all. Adèle is smoking her first cigarette leaning out the window, it's drizzling and I finish drinking my coffee while shaving which I find rather bold of me. The scene reminds me of a similar one in a book I published not long ago whose title and author have slipped my mind and then of Antoine Doinel in love with Mme Tabard standing in front of his mirror though I must grant you that I'm substantially more substantial than Jean-Pierre Léaud. The coffee's getting cold and the smell of shaving cream makes it taste quite disgusting.

My telephone jiggles on the table. It's Meunier's first text of the day. To tell me that Robert Coover's manuscript has landed in Paris and a decision needs to be made fast. It's only just eight o'clock and the office has already sunk its teeth in my ankle. So the morning will start with reading a manuscript. I quite like Coover, he gets on my nerves. He's one of those writers who won't let you read comfortably. He doesn't sell

but I quite like him all the same. I'm sure Meunier is crossing his fingers that I'll turn it down. I'll take it.

I remember that when I met Adèle (she looked like a small black cat in those days) and I was still a very young publisher, I said that if I ever got to publish a book I adored by a gorgeous writer whose work I loved with passion and if the said book got rave notices, was translated into six languages and flew off the bookshelves, then I would drop the job straight away.

All those things have come to pass in the course of time, but never at the same time for the same book. So I go on.

This morning I take 749 strides to get to work and do some good to myself.

6

Coover's manuscript has been put on my desk. Some fair hand has shifted all the other paperwork to the sides so the Coover is fully centred, in case I should take it into my head to bury it beneath one of my towering piles, my paper Eiffels and Etihads. I suddenly have a vision of what my office will be like some day soon: blank. Just a small black screen on a fine piece of walnut burr. Empty shelves waiting to be dismantled. No smell apart from my own. Might there be some vintage photos of books on the walls? Kertész, perhaps? Starlets with haystack hairdos pretending to read a Penguin? But there won't be any manuscript mountains or any piles of snail mail stuck in front of the computer keyboard. Just yellow Post-its with felt-tip reminders from Sabine: "Remember to stop ordering paper", "Don't forget to stop calling in at the printers", "Remember to go to the binder's funeral", "Don't forget not to turn down the corners of the pages", "Remember not to throw books at the wall, not even really awful ones", "Don't forget to keep a real book and a spare candle in your drawer in case of a power cut", "Remember to be the anti-you".

My chair squeaks as I fling my feet onto a pile of literary supplements from *Le Monde*. The Coover. It's a collection

of short stories. That'll be right up Meunier's street, as it'll allow him to bore me with his theory of unsaleability again. I'll build my case for Coover on his belonging to ELO, the Electronic Literature Organization. A man of the future, a modern postmodernist. He's won the Faulkner, that'll calm Meunier down. He's like my butcher, Roger, who salivates over prize-winning cows. He decorates his shop window with their trophies.

I batten down my hatches. I see nothing, I hear nothing, I just read. Coover is a difficult writer. You have to find your own way through his defences. You may get a few blisters on your hands and bumps on your elbows and knees as you push through, but once you're in, you have the wonderful, uncomfortable treat of reading that's worth reading.

It may not be my favourite kind of writing, but it's the kind that brings my critical habits to a halt. There can be no question of not publishing him. We'll have to get a top-flight translator, Bernard Hoepffner or Jean-Yves Pétillon or someone like that. "So how much extra is that going to cost?" When the Meuniers of this world inserted money into "my" firm, they also brought war. Or at least a war game. As I'm the one who's already lost and who will lose overall in any case, I've retained the right to score lots of minor local victories. The parts are all set and the handle of the dagger can already be seen sticking out of my back. Meanwhile, I publish good books that last a few hours, some of which go to slumber on the shelves of major libraries and most of which are turned back into paper. Before they get turned

back into pixels. How will they go about pulping readers? I've always liked books more than money, alas.

I go for Meunier's jugular. He's barely poked his nose round my door when I bawl out loud:

"The Coover's fan-bloody-tastic! A gem! Maminard will go green in the face when they find out it's been stolen from under their noses. No time to lose! Take out an option, draw up the contract, get the translators on the job. We'll be on the front page of *Libération* with a book like this! On the eight o'clock television news! It's wild! Solid gold."

"So how many will it sell?"

"That's something you'll have to ask Meunier, old pal! If he's any good, Meunier will sell a truckload. Am I wrong, Meunier?"

"Let me have a look… Short stories? We'll talk about this later on. You have to come with me right now."

"Where to?"

"You know full well it's the retirement party for M Marcel and Mlle Mathilde, after forty years' simulated sterling service."

"Wasn't that for tomorrow?"

"The tooter the sweeter."

Mlle Mathilde is instantly identifiable. She's the old lady dabbing her eyes with a tiny embroidered handkerchief. She's sniffling and blushing. Mlle Mathilde never was much

fun, I probably hired her in a depression, but she was a good book-keeper of the old kind who made a column of sums received on one side and a column of sums paid on the other and bit her nails to the bone when there was the slightest discrepancy between them. The carpets of the office have been well watered with Mlle Mathilde's tears. They will never dry. She was so keen to see the first column go on longer than the second one! The whole staff is in attendance around her, and she has a last good cry over French publishing and over poor M Dubois. Meunier is standing to attention among his crowd of clones, who are already honing their fangs in pursuit of the soon-to-be-empty office space. Valentine keeps in the background, she gives me a friendly wink and nods her chin towards her fellow interns. They've sequestered all the peanuts, they're hungry. M Marcel, the stock manager, chief book packer and unpacker (the backbone of the trade, and its short-term future) knows what he's up to. This is just a rite of passage preparing him to rise to the high plateau of pétanque and pastis, where real life begins.

To play my part and round things off I drone on interminably with recollections of great events, mentions of great writers, festive evenings at the bar of Hôtel Lutetia when one of them was on Bernard Pivot's television show, the runaway success that obliged us to buy in extra paper from our competitors, the extraordinary delights of the profession, the day when Mlle Mathilde made an arithmetical mistake, the day when M Marcel went to fetch Jean d'Ormesson from his château at Blois, the three fat years when Mlle Mathilde

had to overcome her inborn aversion to making me sign out annual bonuses because we had made so much lovely money. I cleverly avoided mentioning the mass landing of grey suits who had given Mlle Mathilde the shakes and driven her to Prozac and I concluded with a flourish of bonhomie by recalling the times when Mlle Mathilde shared her jar of pickled gherkins with M Marcel during lunch breaks. We drank, we ate and some went away into retirement. "Oof," said Meunier, drily.

At the end of the jollification I motioned Valentine to follow me back to my office.

"You're looking very smart. It's the first time I've seen you in a skirt and cardigan. You must have a dinner date with Meunier, at least?"

"Almost!"

"If it's not with him, then it's with his clone."

"Bulls-eye!"

"You're going to have a ball... I just wanted to tell you something urgent. Have you started reading the manuscript I gave you?"

"Yes, but..."

"No pressure, take it at your own pace, but I wanted to tell you two things you need to know when you're reading for work: you have to learn to read and judge things you don't like. An ordinary reader can dump his book before it's too late or leave it on a bench in the Métro, but you can't do that now. You have to plough on to the end with an even mind,

and put it back on the pile without emotion. The other thing is an unavoidable exercise of the imagination: you have to keep in mind how the text will look when it's been made into a book. When it's in print, it suddenly becomes something weightier. Printing and binding work wonders for some texts; for other texts, it doesn't make a huge difference. My tips won't be of the slightest utility for running concerts, and they won't be any use to publishers of the future, but I had to let you have them before I go home to retire tonight, or some other evening."

7

I'm keeping an oblique eye on Geneviève as we sit face to face in the railway carriage. I'm pretending to read a manuscript on my tablet, whereas she appears to be doing nothing at all. I know she'll not say a word until we get to our destination. Every time I go on tour with her for a book signing we follow the same identical routine. She gazes with blind concentration at the scenery, letting her head sway to the beat of the train, and sometimes she shuts her eyes for a minute and takes a deep breath, like an athlete. She's wearing a purple jacket and skirt and a white blouse with a gold brooch. That isn't her style at all, but it's as close as you can get to the generic Middle-Aged Mother of Two she's going to have to twist round her little finger a short while from now. On each of her forays to the smaller cities of France, she devotes her travel time to rewinding. I appreciate these excursions that always begin with these two hours of silence in honour of the French publishing industry.

Geneviève is a born signer. She's never missed a book fair, a reading or a bookshop with more than twenty linear metres of shelving.

This one, the bookshop we're at today, is immense. A cathedral of books three floors high, graced with a phalanx of salesgirls in red tops, a graphic novel section, a cookery section, a table of new releases—a pile of my own, because we're visiting—travel books, crime, and a huge array of the latest fad, chick lit. Pile 'em high is the number one survival strategy for bookshops in the provinces. Number two is coffee. This shop has its own tile-floored café in the middle of the store with small tables and a pastry display shelf.

The lady readers are there. I slip into their midst and would barely be visible if it weren't for the glass of red in my hand. Then Geneviève comes on stage, takes the microphone that someone hands her, starts talking, and just keeps on. She agrees to answer all and any questions from the public and first "Yes, my book is entirely autobiographical" (as if reality was a criterion of literary quality). She possesses the magic formula for hanging on to husbands, despite not having one, she weighs up the respective advantages of clitoral versus vaginal pleasure, her grandmother gave her a slightly different recipe for prune flan, in her view running is worse for the knees than downhill skiing, raising children is a human adventure, the literature of tomorrow will be readable or will not be, levity is a victory over gravity, style is the woman and she's there to prove it, goat cheese is not as rich as Edam, Janine Boissard's books aren't bad at all, yes, of course, Balzac and Maupassant, and how can you leave out Simone de Beauvoir, of course you can read while watching television, I quite agree that reality shows aren't

as real as all that, and there's nothing quite like a good book published by Robert Dubois Books bought from your treasured local bookshop.

I really admire Geneviève. I admire the readers who turn up every week to ask the touring lady writer if her book really is autobiographical. And Geneviève signs, and signs. What was your first name? And your husband's?

Do I do my work for these readers? Objectively, I do. But don't I really do it for a kind of ideal reader I dream of but whose mould was broken long ago? I sincerely admire Geneviève for underselling her work day in and day out, because she's worth twenty times more than what she pretends to be. Geneviève is a real writer, I wouldn't publish her if she weren't, but she gave up saying so a long time ago. Life has taught her to keep quiet about it.

A timid young woman comes up to me with her hands behind her back. I've guessed it already: she's written a book and she'd like to take the opportunity… It's about a boy, you see, and he meets a girl… Every trip has its haul.

The bookseller has gone off to a family do, the readers have flown back to their nests and Geneviève has gone up to her room for a moment. I'm waiting for her on the sofa in the lobby and leafing through the young woman's manuscript without reading it. I feel I'm far from the office, far from Paris, but does that mean I am nearer to anything else? I call Adèle and she clears her throat to say she thinks I'm a brave man to carry on doing the rounds. I reply that I don't

know what she's talking about and I read her an occasional poem I made up in my head while Geneviève was talking. It's a quatrain called "Barbara":

> *The rain's stopped in Brest*
> *But you'll get no rest*
> *They're building a tram*
> *In Rue de Siam*

Geneviève comes out of the lift in a jangle of keys. She's her old self once again. In slacks and high heels, with a slinky sweater made to showcase her mammary glands and an embroidered jacket with pendants that sparkle and clink. She's wearing make-up, and has put up her hair. She's large, colourful and noisy.

She takes me by the arm and pulls me along, she absolutely MUST eat on a boat she knows where you get soles as thick as Camus's *Outsider*.

"Well, I'm not too good with boats…"

"This one won't upset you, it's got a lead bottom and it can't sink or swim! You silly old landlubber!"

"You were spot on at the bookshop."

"Stop harassing me, will you?"

We walk along the riverside path. Night is falling and in the half-light she tells me the story of the book by Châteaureynaud she's reading and is thrilled by.

I listen, but what surprises me is our being alone together. It's been a long while. Usually she always drags a young bookseller along with us, or a journalist. It strikes me that a young sailor in service whites, like in *Querelle of Brest*, would complement the scenery quite well this evening.

The boat turns out to be quite pleasant. No rolling or pitching. It smells of old wood, fresh fish and melted butter. Geneviève has to bend her long neck quite low to avoid bumping herself on the ceiling. She calls for muscadet and winkles to nibble before the sole is served. I go for a dozen Pacific oysters and cod cooked with lentils and diced bacon.

"Are you writing anything at the moment?"

"I am always writing something. I'm a tree and I make leaves."

"Sap rising?"

"I think so."

"Is it a mystery?"

"No, it'll be a book. The story of a girl who meets a man…"

"You'll have a hard time pretending it's autobiographical!"

"What a boor you are! You are perfectly aware what I can do and no less aware what my book will be like."

"Trademarked Geneviève. Can I give you an oyster?"

"I'm really enjoying being here alone with you. It's a lovely evening."

8

"And the sole on your plate is lovely too."

"Please fillet it for me. I've always loved watching you in the kitchen. The way you handle food makes me hungry. I'm going to miss you, Robert."

"What was that? You'll miss me?"

"I meant to tell you that I'm going to give the book I'm working on to Brasset. As a publisher he has his flops, I know, but he's more into television than you are and I need to get my foot in that door."

"You're over twenty per cent of my gross, you know."

"And you're a hundred per cent of mine. I need to earn more money."

"I'm leaving the small bones on the rim of your plate. You can suck them, they're dripping with butter."

Valentine is so excited she can hardly get the words out.

"I've finished reading the manuscript and it's very good. I made an effort like you told me, to read what I didn't like, but I really like it. I could be wrong, but the story is touching. The heroine is a girl and she meets a guy…"

"Stop there. I know the rest."

"Have you read it?"

"I've read it a hundred times if I've read it once. I trust you. Do you think it's well written?"

"It kept me turning the pages, at any rate. What are you going to do?"

"Nothing… You are going to call the author and tell her that her manuscript has been accepted."

"But I don't know how to do that! I'm an intern."

"Interns are the people who keep French publishing alive, or so I'm told. So get on with it!"

"She'll never believe me."

"Tell her you're a intern doing a 'good news' training course, and that the job you have is the nicest part of the whole trade. Don't skimp on enthusiasm. If she takes her book anywhere else, I'll wring your neck."

"She's going to want a contract, an undertaking, I don't know what else."

"She'll get. But first of all she'll have a good news call from Valentine."

As I speak I stroke my tablet, which is on my desktop but not switched on. I catch myself doing that from time to time. My reader has the feel of dark chocolate.

"By the way, how did your dinner with the clone go?"

"He slavers."

"Slavers?"

"I mean, like he's really greedy. But I must say he's well into German rock."

"Did you get anything out of him?"

"I didn't understand all of it, but he seems to be cooking up quite a stew with Meunier."

"Those guys certainly know how to stir a pot."

"Do you like him, Meunier, I mean?"

"Do I have a choice? Are you going to go out with the guy again?"

"Sure. We're going to a concert on Saturday."

"At any rate you look better in your orange polka-dot skirt than in your granny suit. It's more you."

"Alright, I'll go and make the call. How do you address a writer?"

"By name. Writers, broadly speaking, are human beings."

"Even Bret Easton Ellis?"

To cap it all, Balmer is really there, for once. He's sitting at my table, with his napkin already spread over his paunch, looking jolly and sly. The spitting image of the books he writes. He's having a great palaver with Mme Martin. He's put his iPhone on the tablecloth but keeps it under the flat of his hand.

"Watch out, if you let her go on she'll inveigle you into ordering her disgusting duck with orange, and if you eat that in front of me, I'll file for divorce."

"I'm warning you, if we divorce, I keep the children."

"Good riddance."

"If I have leeks vinaigrette and lentils with salt pork, will you still pay the bill?"

"I concur about the leeks, but I'll have sole to follow. I need to come to terms with sole. As for the bill I don't have a choice. Bouzy."

"Was that a recommendation?"

"That was an order. So how are you, cyberwriter?"

"I'm having a whale of a time, believe you me. While you lot scratch heads and scrape barrels trying to find ways of selling old-style novels online without upsetting the booksellers you'll end up killing off anyway, we're churning out new stuff that slips into these little toys all by itself."

"Yes, but you're the king of constraint."

"The prince of freedom, my dear man."

"What about the others?"

"Other people will either do the same as us, or carry on with what they did before. There will always be paper and there will always be screens. Pages don't turn in one fell swoop."

"What exactly is it that you're doing?"

"Redacted! Nincompoop! You can't expect me to give away what I'm up to. Relax, the leeks are good."

"I can't imagine what she puts in her fucking vinaigrette. After all these years I really should have worked it out. Are you going to finish your book all the same? Don't leave me high and dry, I want it for my September list."

"You'll get it. I'm still up to producing old books the way you like them. I'll have it finished soon."

"I'm looking forward to reading it."

"Well, I'm not looking forward to one thing, and that's signing a contract with you. I've no intention of ceding electronic rights for almost nothing. The rights you can't be bothered to exploit, but still want to have for a dime."

"That's Meunier."

"I don't give a damn if it's you or Meunier, all I know is that I'm being robbed. Mind over matter, my foot! Using hard-copy rights as a template is pretending things are staying the same, whereas everything is changing as we speak. For creative people, you're a bit pathetic. Sell two hundred thousand print copies first, then we can talk."

"Well, don't sign. Strike out the clause and retain your rights. Do you think your cyber-heroes are going to turn themselves into publishers?"

"If they make texts available to readers, they can't be far off."

"I'd like you to do me a favour: can you fillet my sole?"

"Got a sore hand?"

Balmer is the most gifted of the whole lot. He has all the talents. He works it all out before he sets pen to paper and so when he appears to be freewheeling, he's actually deep in thought. He is the model of the perfect, adaptable, intransigent writer, always identical and never the same. He can take criticism and turn it to his advantage. An inventor of form and content. (Didn't I hear they had a lot to do with each other?) He is the real reason I do the job that I do. He

makes me proud to be me. I've been his publisher for twelve years now, and readers have just noticed. This morning he's wearing stubble, he's probably not really woken up yet. He casts an anxious glance at his phone, wondering which of his girlfriends is going to get first call on him. He is also the only man in town with enough understanding to fillet my sole without asking questions. He tackles the job as if he had flippers for hands, to boot. He'd like to be certain I really did read the article in *Le Monde* about his latest book.

"That was last night's close reading."

9

I've decided to take my dear reader out for a walk. I want it to see the world.

First comes the pocket test, which it fails miserably. It's too big for the side pocket in my jacket, it's too rigid to be stuffed into the slant pocket in my raincoat, and it would be simply futile to try to slide it into the inside pocket of my jacket. Even if it were small enough for that location, it would make me look as if I had Weissmuller's pecs, and its blunt edges would inevitably shred the lining in no time. You can forget about trouser pockets: given the weight of the thing, you'd soon find yourself on the street in flower-patterned underpants with your trousers round your ankles. Unless you also wore broad and sturdy braces... And when you think "braces", you think "holster". Might an adapted police model fit the bill? On the other hand, you can't deny that a reader is somewhat more rectangular in shape than a Colt 45. I shall have to submit this sartorial problem to my tailor, Mr Hollington, who specializes in clothing the edito-architectural clan by providing its members with pipe-pockets, phone-pockets and cigarette-pockets, alongside special places for fold-out rulers, all kinds of pencils and pens, not to mention hip-flasks. For

the time being, however, let us concede that the reader is an awkward customer, and that we shall need to raise from his grave some publishing genius who can reinvent the paperback version as well as the wheel.

However, it comes through the park-reading test with flying colours. I squeeze between the Arnys shop front and the *terrasse* of the Récamier (an old publishers' restaurant that's moved on to politicians and prices that go with) and then settle down in the little garden at the end of the street, out of range of buildings and noise. The reader works when I lay it on my lap (legs crossed), when I hold it in both hands, when I hold it in one hand, when I lay it on the bench beside me (18-point font) and when it's in the shadow of a plane tree. I imagine that if one of the countless pigeons that shit over Paris aimed at the screen it would do no greater damage than it would to a book—and maybe less. Remember to keep a packet of tissues handy just in case. I spy a passing sunbeam between the rooftops and when it lands near me I adjust my position so it falls directly on the screen. The light war is a hopeless cause. Even if I put brightness to max, I can't read a thing. But what would Baudelaire have read in the noonday sun?

Restaurant reading must be easier in small towns than in Paris and easier in some parts of the right bank than in Saint-Germain-des-Prés. The size of the tables coupled with the size of the plates makes it hard to put the reader down. Is the reader up to a glass of wine? What effect would a mouthful of red have on Proust?

Reading while walking is not to be recommended in any case. It would only be worth the risk if you were deep into a truly extraordinary text. Reading poetry, on the other hand, is better suited to circumperambulation, you can raise your glance at the end of a line to keep a look-out for passing pillars and lamp-posts.

It works fine in a café. Espresso cups are small, and lebensraum a less crucial concern. The level of light is perfect, the ambient hubbub is easily cancelled out, and you can get down to serious business. Note-taking on a reader is a disaster. I hate it. I can manage the keyboard perfectly well, but what I can do with it doesn't suit me. What I like about notes in the margin is the gulf between the text and the note. I use a pencil and scribble away at speed, so my notes are the polar opposite of print. They don't constrain the text in any way, they aren't in competition with it, they aren't like it at all. They're addressed to the writer more than to the writing. But on the reader these fully formed inserts scare me, they look like imperial commands. I'd like to write directly onto the screen with a magic marker.

Valentine is tapping at the window of the café. I beckon her to come in.

"Am I interrupting?"

"Coffee?"

"No thanks. I've got another question."

On which more anon.

When my reader suddenly winks and asks me to plug it in, I grasp it by the lead and go over to the bar. The waiter knows what I'm after.

"Could you plug me in, please? I'm running out."

He grins back at me.

"Have a heart. I can't wait to find out if Lisbeth Salander is going to get out of trouble. They're treating her terribly. They want to eliminate her and the journalist hasn't got in touch… She's been bashed up something dreadful, and I'm scared…"

"Has it occurred to you what would happen to me if every scaredy-cat in the vicinity came and sucked the electricity out of my meter? You pay for your own petrol, don't you?"

"I'll pay up."

"But we don't have juice on the price list yet. Safer for you to go and plug yourself in at home. You could also buy the paperback to find out how the story ends. By coincidence, I've got one here, under the counter. Customers leave them lying around. Here you are. Isn't that the one? It's taken a beating, but the story must still be inside."

I've arranged to meet Adèle at the bar of Hôtel Lutetia in the late afternoon. I'd almost forgotten what it used to be like, when for one part of my life I had to be there almost constantly to mingle with colleagues male and female, with writers and producers, and when it was also imperative to find a quiet nook so the contract under discussion wouldn't be

broadcast immediately to all and sundry and also to head off gossip and insinuations about affairs and deals between you and the person you were with. But now the old timers have gone: the Cromlech has retired, Tenterhooks has moved out, and the Stone Commander has died. Some of the losses break my heart, some I am really sorry about, others not so much.

I nod to Dussolier, who's a regular, place two pecks on the capacious cheeks of fat Fanfan, and here I am slumped in a red armchair opposite Adèle who's already got a whisky to pick her up.

"Imagine I wanted to lend you a book," says I. "If I give you my reader, not only do I have nothing left to read myself, but, knowing you, I'd be afraid you'd read another one of the books inside it. What is to be done?"

"That's not a problem. You buy me a reader (you should have done that ages ago, by the way) and you use the drainpipe plugin to pour the book you want to lend me from your reader into mine. It's soft and silky and, I must say, rather sexy."

"The method, you mean? Or me, myself?"

I O

Valentine has finally managed to round them all up in my office. I say all, but I think there must be many more interns in the firm and these constitute just one squad. They look the part: they're wearing jeans on their lower halves, black sweaters on their uppers and are unshaven (by my standards). There are three lads and her, which seems obvious to me: three lads and a polychrome her in a red skirt and yellow stockings that match her top.

"This is Gregor, who's at Sciences Po, that's Sam out of Normale Sup', and here's Kevin, the geek."

"Geek out of where?"

"Technical college."

They hold their peace for a moment. They're not too sure what I expect of them. They stare at me and, since I say nothing, the one called Sam kicks off.

"Is it true you let Valentine acquire a manuscript and call the author to tell her she'd been accepted?"

"Excuse me, I chose the manuscript for Valentine to read. Apart from that detail, it's all true. You read, you like, you publish and you sell. That's what publishing is about, don't you think?"

"So you cross your fingers and hope readers will like it as well?"

"That would be too easy, comrade. There's nothing wrong with crossing your fingers, but no way can you just sit back. The job goes on, you could even say that's where it begins. When the book comes back from production, Valentine will have to talk to journalists, sales reps, booksellers, friends and Facebook. She'll have to make a splash and do a lot of stroking as well, run the whole gamut… If she does it properly, then in ten years' time, if her author goes on writing, she'll have name recognition, she'll get mentioned in newspapers, on radio, in blogs. She'll have created her own family of readers, who'll look out for her books and read them. The unknown factor is the size of that family. There are writers with very loyal families that are small, even tiny. Some have large, capricious families that come and go. And then there are the ones with vast families, who have to be careful to cook up just the right meal for every baby shower."

Upon which, while I'm still talking, I put my foot in it. Using my Victorinox I open a bottle of pic saint-loup for them. I chose that wine because it's not yet settled into a definitive shape. You can pick up bottles of it that are frankly poor, you can find much more expensive ones that are hardly any better, and quite often ones in full bloom with features that are gradually establishing themselves. It's a wine for the emergent connoisseur. An adolescent vintage. But I've put my foot in it because they ask in unison if I haven't got any

beer. Yes, I have no beer. They'll wet their lips with my wine all the same, albeit without enthusiasm.

As I imagine Valentine has already had a word with them I don't wait to get to the end of my glass before saying:

"So?"

"So," says Kevin. "We've already managed to clear off the shelves a fair bit of hard copy clutter: *Who's Who*, Cook's Railway Timetable, *Encyclopaedia Universalis*, almost the entire mail-order catalogue, and we'll soon be on to newspapers… We've done a fair bit of work…"

"Don't mind him, Kevin's other name is *tabula rasa*. He's a screen-only geek! I don't care about the channel, I'm keener on games and what you can do with them. They're already great and as they develop they are bound to turn into literature…"

"Let's take it in steps. What do you like to read?"

"What I would like, myself," says Valentine, "is to get a nice poem every morning on my iPhone and an episode of a made-for-the-métro serial complete with pictures of the bad guy and the poor good-looking blonde, plus some music in the buds. For the rest of the day I've got an iPad and a laptop, and in the evening I'd like to have a good old printed book for when I collapse into bed."

"What I'm interested in is whatever you can come up with by way of new kinds of material for screen reading. We really should have had Perec on board. We need to exploit it to exhaustion and try out anything and everything, getting

as far as we can from forms that owe their existence to print. Fiction may turn out to be on the losing side, poetry is going to benefit, short forms as well, super-heavy stuff, irreverent stuff, blogs and who knows what we can imagine coming over the horizon…"

"The first thing is, we take the writer and the text apart. Smash them up. Make them do something else. Mix them up…"

"Invent mass-market e-Bookers."

"Put the skates on kid's schoolbags…"

I take a deep mouthful of pic saint-loup. Now it's been open for a while it's got really rather velvety. That's a pity. The four of them are sitting opposite me. They're huddled together for safety. They're a funny bunch. I'm going to do something to throw them into the lion's den of life. They'll not even have time to be scared.

"So I've got an idea: let's create our own start-up, our own company, and get on with the job."

"But the publishing house exists already…"

"Irrelevant! It'll just be the five of us. Top secret!"

"It takes money!"

"I think that will be my role in the start-up. I'll put up the cash and you put in everything else. On one condition: you don't waste any time on the channel. That includes you, geek. You work exclusively on what's going to be channelled. Texts, ideas, pix, writers, just the writers. Turn every stone to

find them, turn yourselves into writers, whatever you like, as long as we get content. Everyone's struggling to get old stuff down new tubes. People like Meunier are spending millions doing it. But as we've got nothing, we're going to make new stuff, stuff that's not like anything…"

"And if we have a flop?"

"We will have a flop. Given the nature of the project, we are going to have lots of flops."

"Two steps forward, one step back."

"You said it, Big Chief."

"How do we start?"

"First of all, you find a name for your start-up, I'll deal with the paperwork, and then we get down to business. Actually, you could start on it right now."

"We'll scour the blogs."

"As you wish. Give me a list of everything you'll need."

"How do we square it with this place?"

"How should I know? Anyway, if Meunier takes advantage of you, you could distract him with a spot of industrial action, couldn't you? A collective protest? A work-to-rule?"

On which they glance at each other and huddle even tighter together. I can see the shadow of a profound misgiving pass over them. French publishing is on the march and it's scared. There will be fireworks soon.

"Now, off you go! And don't stop until you've scooped the top off the cream."

11

With her curly red hair done up like a flaming haystack, Sabine is a raging volcano at lunch. Her brown eyes have turned black, and she's spitting sulphurous flames at Meunier.

"You can't let him go on like this. The firm is yours, it's ours, and he's got to be stopped. He refused to sign the contract for our new girl this morning, he sent Balmer packing because he wouldn't sign the amendment on digital rights, and he's hired two more goons in logistics. Where will it all end?"

"Calm down, Sabine, otherwise the very silent Mme Martin will throw us out of the restaurant. We'll talk it all over quietly during lunch. I'll be having veal pâté and skate wing in caper sauce."

"I'm not even hungry."

"I'm really sorry."

"Alright, duck salad and tripe sausage."

"You see, you're feeling better already."

Mme Martin draws near with the bouzy in hand. She puts the bottle on the table, draws the cork, fills the glasses, and sits down.

"The service has gone haywire! I've been coming here for thirty years, and this is the first time I've ever seen you sitting down."

"Nothing's gone haywire, because there's nothing doing. I wanted to tell you personally that I've sold out. I'm closing down."

"Let me guess," Sabine butts in. "Prada? Ralph Lauren? Gucci? Saks?"

"No, it'll carry on as a restaurant."

She turns round, grabs a glass from the next table, and pours herself some bouzy.

"Organic home-style ham sandwiches on rye with carbon-neutral greens on the side?"

"No, it's been bought by some Chinese who are going to do Japanese food."

"Sushi for the smart set!"

"How can you let that happen? After mountains of blanquette, Everests of salt pork and cathedrals of blood sausage and mashed potatoes! You're condemning us to blobs of sticky rice with wafer-thin whitefish toppings! For a king's ransom, of course."

"You'll be able to go on your diet, M Dubois."

"What I'm definitely going to go on is a long walk, to find another decent eatery… I really enjoyed coming here, didn't you know?"

"I believe I did notice. I'll miss you, and your authors too. They were a lot of fun."

"Not all of them. Are you leaving town?"

"I haven't decided. I'm a bit scared of the countryside, and I don't like the city much any more."

"I can see you've got an easy decision coming up."

She gets up and goes with sprightly stride to fetch the food from the kitchen.

"Anything wrong?" Sabine asks. "You've come over quite pale."

"No, nothing wrong. Just my regular one o'clock heart attack."

"Have a drink."

Sabine doesn't know everything about the firm's business, but she's gifted with second sight. She's got a lot of the facts in hand and can put two and two together. I'm annoying her. She can't quite divine what game I'm playing, which makes her feel all at sea and on the side. She wants to know what I'm really up to.

"You can see what's going on. You realize you're being shoved aside and soon you'll be out on the street…"

"Well, now you come to mention it, it's true I can feel the push from time to time. I've even got a bruise, right there."

"You just make jokes about it. Do you really know what's going on behind your back? All his garbage about your being the best publisher in the world, all his sweet-talk at the readers' panel and calling you Gaston—it's only to shore up his own position in the firm. You can see he's taking more and more

of the decisions that rightly belong to you: he selects titles without telling the panel, and he won't sign contracts for titles you've picked."

"So far, I've made him change his mind every time."

"So far. Did you know he's bought Goérand's useless half-baked proposal?"

She takes my reader—"You really ought to clean it! Look at that screen, it's disgusting, you couldn't even read *Night Flight* on it!"—then taps and scrolls to locate the text I'd missed.

"That's one I didn't notice," I say.

"Your shelves are badly arranged. But it's too late. He also offered to double Geneviève's advance. She sent him packing without mentioning it to you."

"She's going to Brasset. Meunier heard that from me."

"She's going to Brasset and you're not lifting a finger?"

"She's looking for something we can't provide."

"So how will we look at the end of the year if we don't have a new title from Geneviève for the book-buying season? Are we going to manufacture a second Geneviève?"

"That could take time."

"Poach other writers?"

"It's not the best time for doing that. Wiser to wait until the prize season is over. Runners-up often feel like a change of publisher. Especially if the winner was from their own stable."

"In sum, we sit on our hands…"

*

Mme Martin draws near and Sabine stops talking.

"One tripe sausage and a skate wing for you, M Dubois."

"When exactly are you closing down, Mme Martin?"

"At the end of the month."

"Are you going to have a going-away party?"

"Certainly not."

"What about the employees?"

"Only one of the waitresses is staying on. The chef refused to convert to teriyaki. He's looking around for another position. *Bon appétit.*"

Sabine takes a *pomme sarladaise*—a slice of potato sautéed in goose fat—from her plate with her fingers and pops it in her mouth. It's burning hot.

"I need to know what you plan to do to put things right."

"You're well aware that nobody has a clue any more as to how things would be if they were put back straight. Two years down the road, who knows if there'll be any bookshops left in France, or if there'll be any solvent paper mills, or whether printers won't be selling their Camerons for scrap and writers turning out drabbles in 6pt Times in English and publishers lining up for a job at Microsoft or Amazon. Begging."

"So what? I'm still alive and I still need to read and work. What's a boss for if it isn't to solve those kinds of problems, to see things coming and to work out how to cope with

them? Now is the time to show you've got some imagination. I used to be convinced you'd got more than your fair share of it. Surprise us, instead of getting rolled over by the men with no minds of their own. You could at least keep up with your interns! They've begun some kind of work to rule that's driving Meunier up the wall. They've launched a campaign of asking questions all the time. Before they do anything at all, they grill him why do we do this and what's the reason for that. It's more effective than a sit-in and it's a clever way of accumulating a huge amount of information without anyone noticing. They'll know all the ins and outs of the business very soon. Follow their lead! You shouldn't be the one to drop the ball by mistake."

12

The night is dark as pitch and its blackness so dense you could touch it. At three thirty the dark and the silence are at their peak. I'm sitting on the sofa with my reader in my lap, but I haven't summoned up the energy to push the on button and make it deliver up text. What's inside it is a menace to me. I resent my profession for having always prevented me from reading what matters—competent writers and properly constructed texts—in favour of drafts, book proposals, blueprints and things that aren't fully finished. Unripe, underdone, without shape or form. In service of a future I shall never see and which will presumably call me a bad chooser who picked the wrong texts, the wrong men, the wrong women. That's what the future is for.

I stretch out legs that feel like lead weights and snuggle down. What will my authors be like in ten years' time? How will life reshape them? How will the best of them reshape life?

One day my phone rang at three thirty in the morning. In those days I was asleep. One of my authors was on the line, beside himself, in a mad whirl. He bellowed into my ear that he'd done it, he'd changed sex, he'd just screwed a

woman, she was right beside him and could testify to it. I've made it, he said, I'm heterosexual now, I'm respectable and I can go on Bernard Pivot's television show! Which he was keen to confirm by coming to the office at break of day. To mark his conversion he'd unearthed an old and faded check suit that was too tight for him, complemented by a green tie such as only a man who never wears ties could possibly select.

"Look, I'm presentable. You can call the man, Pivot I mean, you can tell him I'm OK, I don't put bombs in dustbins any more, and I fuck women."

"You're looking great, I really mean it, but I don't think that fronting as a straight man with a tie will be a lot of use. Not if you want to promote a book that deals exclusively with homosexuality, and does it very well."

"But you could take me out for lunch with him to get him on side, I promise I'll behave myself. If I get on the television book programme my whole life will change, I'll have them in stitches, and we'll make a fortune. Have I got things to tell the viewers!"

"Write them down."

"But people don't read anything any more! That's all over!"

For all the years that it lasted, I heard the same question from all my authors: When do I get my turn on Pivot's TV show? Being on the show gave you the magic badge of authorness. It made you a writer in the eyes of the world and of the corner store salesgirl. A whole long week of fame and recognition.

I'm a writer, at last! Yet they'd spent all their days and nights doing nothing but write.

An early retiree from the teaching profession—presumably a French teacher—was sitting opposite me in my office one day. She had an impeccable hairdo, and was dressed and accessorized in like manner. She handed me a wad of paper.

"Here's my manuscript. I'm sure it will need revision, and please don't take offence at the mistakes, because I wrote it at top speed as soon as I'd retired so as to get on Pivot's show before I look too decrepit."

"Do you mean that you wrote it *in order* to be on Pivot's show?"

"Isn't that what everyone does?"

Adèle, who always had a crush on Pivot and still does, told me she'd once talked him into hosting one of her favourite authors. The writer in question was an academic grandee of the kind we no longer make, as well as being a polished stylist and a brilliant speaker. He entranced his students, bewitched his colleagues and his publisher, and clearly enthused his publicist as well. When the chattering classes heard that he was going to appear on *Apostrophes*, it was a no-brainer that we would have a tidal wave of the kind Vincenot launched when in fifteen minutes flat he'd charmed the whole of France and created a vast new market for regional writing. Pivot himself was glad to have such a distinguished and mildly demanding author on his show, such a fine figure of

a writer too. He swept his forelock to one side, and over his half-moon spectacles asked his first question. Whereupon our great writer went out like a light. Overwhelmed by what was at stake and by everybody's expectations, not to mention his own, he mumbled and stumbled. The only expression that could be made out on his face was as if to say, "What the hell am I doing here? Get me out as fast as you can!" Pivot moved on to the guest sitting next to him, who had nothing to say, but did so agreeably.

Writers had high hopes of the conversation they could undertake in a single evening with millions of viewers who might become readers. It was a legitimate expectation; at that time television was a gift to books and writers wanted to take advantage of it. But now that television is a gift to television alone, writers are all over the place. They go in search of their readers one by one, they tour primary schools, secondary schools, colleges, conferences, and French cultural centres overseas. Their knees are giving out and their carbon footprint is disastrous.

Just one of my authors who had correctly understood the workings of the Society of Spectacle made me put a clause in his contract stipulating that he would never be required to appear on Pivot's show—which was the best way of making everyone else want to have him. But he maintained a stolid indifference to all media requests. Obviously Pivot never expressed the least wish to have him appear, depriving me of the pleasure of saying no to someone to whom the whole world was eager to say yes.

I decide to switch my reader on. The glare jumps out at me. The brightness is set to daytime. I tone it down to the night setting and read. I slowly fall under its spell. It's a very good text and I sail through it effortlessly. It's about a cat in the Marais district and I suspect it's loaded with narrative dynamite but for the time being I lap it up as if it was a story about a cat in the Marais district of Paris.

I can hear a noise in the bedroom. The bed creaks. Adèle is getting up. She comes into the lounge all woozy with sleep.

"I'm thirsty, I can't sleep."

She vanishes into the kitchen, wearing nothing but a tee shirt, showing her buttocks, and comes back more awake with a glass in her hand, showing her pubis. She's lost weight.

"Do you want a drink as well? It's hot. Have a sip of mine. Make room for me next to you and switch the light on. You scare me with your reader under your chin. You are not a ghost. You are a publisher."

13

The publishing house is silent. Everyone has abandoned ship. It's the hour when Gregor, Sam and Kevin furtively poke their noses round my office door.

"Come in, come in, this time I have some beer."

"I'd rather stand," says Kevin. "I think better and the beer goes down faster."

"Pscht," say the ring pulls.

"So, we've had a good think," Sam begins.

"Aren't we going to wait for Valentine before getting stuck into it?"

"Valentine's gone."

"What do you mean, gone?"

"Yeah, she got a job at the Crécy Bang, the electro house festival out in the suburbs. In the strawberry fields."

"So she's left publishing, has she? But I've still got her list of questions on my desk. It seemed like she'd got interested in the job. What's more, she's leaving me to deal with her new author Maud. Is that kind of behaviour typical of her?"

"You know, blacks only go in for lolly and rock. Schmatters as well, up to a point, but the main thing is the beat, right?"

"Write a hundred and fifty pages on those lines and we'll all go to jail. You're on a slippery slope."

"Don't worry, I'm only joking. She needed money and she also wanted to get back together with a guitarist she'd picked up at the country and western festival. A Balkan kind of bloke, I believe. Somewhat scarred and dented."

"As bad as that, is it?"

Which is how I find myself slightly under-equipped to deal with three strapping lads. I realise that I'd never thought of them without Valentine, and that in her absence the plan doesn't have the same shape. Does it have any shape at all? Actually, she was the novelty, the bright idea. She *together with* them. The balance looked right to me. It looked like a team but now, with just three lads, the possible division of labour looks a bit too obvious. I can't quite see where the spark will come from. She could at least have said goodbye.

"So you see," Sam began again with a scratch of his mohawk, "we've found a name for the start-up. Are you going to tell him, Gregor?"

"You go ahead, it was your idea."

"OK, so we want to call it 'Robswood'. Robswood Books. So we keep your name, under a kind of cloak."

"The cloak hides a dagger that helps people pay up."

"We want to be musketeers on the electronic highway."

"I think it's a good name—and very sweet of you too. I've been getting on with the formalities, and now

that I have a name I'll be able to register the articles of association and put in the money. I'll just have to have your signatures on the forms. Then we'll have to reassign duties, now that Valentine's dropped out. Whatever got into her? We're going to miss her. Couldn't you give her a call just to make sure?"

"We ought to leave her alone. She's right."

"Then it occurred to us that as we're getting older," Gregor went on, "we'll bring Kevin's kid brother on board. He's fourteen and super smart. Just the right age for tinkering."

Gregor stands up to retrieve from the rear pocket of his jeans a piece of paper that's been folded in four and moulded to the shape of his buttock. He unfolds and uncreases it and puts it on the coffee table. Since it persists in turning up a corner he keeps it flat with his beer can.

As it turns out I'm quite content to drink a beer with them. It's not my favourite beverage, in any case not when I'm in Paris, but I think we'll have to get used to it and that publishing will have to adjust very quickly. I must remind myself to do the big book of beer cans for next Christmas.

"I've done a quick business plan. We should lose a fair bit at the start, but make plenty when things get going."

"I prefer it that way round. It gives me a warm feeling."

"What has to be paid are the minimum wages, since we've already got the gear and we work from home."

"And you can also nick pencils and paper from here."

"Paper?"

His question makes me burst out laughing, and they stare at me with surprise.

"Excuse me, but I find it very funny to think you don't want any paper, because my own start in the profession was a paper deal. I was editorial director of the firm and as a result of serious complications I became the owner. I was very pleased but as I had a literary background I was scared of getting robbed. My first task as boss was to purchase printing paper. A huge mass of paper, because we had a title that was roaring away and we had to print trainloads of it. I got myself an invitation to talk to the guy who'd given me my first break and had provided me with capital. Old school, upper crust still stuck to the oven. His driver takes us to a stratospheric restaurant he frequented. We sit down, champagne, *mises en bouche*, and I ask him point blank how I should go about negotiating the purchase of several tons of paper. He leans back in his seat and launches into a technical explanation. 'If the man you're dealing with comes from ESSEC business school—you'll soon know, as they can hardly stop themselves telling you—then haggle over the product. Talk about weight, handling, colour, rolls, and so on, and leave price to the end… But if your opposite number is from HEC business school—where they hold money in very high regard—you haggle over price to start with and get down to the technicalities later on.' At that point he paused, took a drink, shifted on his chair and looked me straight in the eye with crossed brow, saying: 'Obviously, if

he's read Balzac's *Lost Illusions* or Maupassant's *Bel-Ami*, it can all come unstuck in a split second. But as you read them before he did, it should all go fine.' That's exactly when I became a publisher."

14

I don't quite understand how they got there, but the business plan and the whole publishing proposal are on my reader already, and I spend the night going through them again. One thing is clear—the lads aren't wolves. Another thing is even clearer—they're enjoying themselves no end. More than half of what they're suggesting seems improbable at best, but I'm dreadfully mistrustful of my own judgment. I balance my tablet unsteadily on my knees. It wobbles for a second and I catch it like a ball just as it's falling off. I have another go. What would happen if it fell? What kind of shatter pattern would appear on the screen if it broke? I'm finding it hard to understand why having Valentine on the team struck me as a reassurance. As if with her brightly coloured skirts, drop dead stockings and black skin she'd been the embodiment of novelty and difference. She was the radical face of Robswood Books. She would have helped me accept the plan as a whole and without reservation.

In the morning I call Balmer.

"Balmer?"

"Robert? How nice of you to call at dawn."

"Get dressed, I'm sending you three lads with lousy hairdos and I forbid you to tell me I'm insane. They're brilliant. Listen to what they have to say. If any of it interests you, quiz them and then tell me sincerely what you think of it all. But keep it strictly to yourself."

"Robert, whatever are you up to now? Couldn't you set me up with a nice full-colour album of pedigree cats for Christmas? Or a lavish *Loire Châteaux* you'd sell to the Americans? You're incorrigible. I'll give your lads a grilling, I think I can see what you're cooking up, but I honestly never thought you'd do it that way."

"So how did you think I would go about it?"

"I imagined you being more inclined towards big guns."

"Meunier is already in the mortar barrel. The calibre isn't big enough for both of us."

"How much latitude do your lads have?"

"To the date-line either way round. They have to be allowed to do stupid things. The main thing is to see if there are any blue flowers poking up between the weeds."

"I'm no stranger to stupid ideas. Beyond that, I'll keep my eyes peeled and let you know… Do I get a fee?"

"A fat one."

I like my office early in the morning. I close my eyes and listen. A furtive accountant slips softly along the corridor, then a secretary, then the receptionist. I can almost hear them yawning and cracking their finger joints. The office is slowly waking up, a few doors bang, there's a first rumble of speech,

the call of a computer being switched on, and suddenly, like a reveille, the smell of coffee. We'll soon be able to start talking.

A steaming "I ♥ NY" mug enters my office followed by Meunier in an open-neck white shirt. Dreadfully awake. He closes the door behind him. It's time for a confidential chat.

"Gaston, I need your help."

"Things must be bad."

"I'm worried about the interns. I think they're dragging their feet."

"Does it matter?"

"There's a fair bit of work to do at present and I'd like to be able to rely on them."

"Aren't they here to learn, not to work?"

"Is not work the best way to learn?"

"In that case, you just have to motivate them the same way you motivate workers, by giving them interesting things to do and huge wads of money."

"I see you're still an expert in magic solutions. I'd like you to see them and give them a pep talk, tell them about the business with loads of anecdotes, the way you know how. Make them see how lucky they are to be here…"

"How they'll be unemployed when they leave here, and how beautiful life is."

"Try to be positive for once, Robert, and please, see them for me."

"That's an order."

*

At that point I go straight back to basics. I dash in to see Emmanuelle, the hinge between editorial and production, at the very heart of the publishing business.

"Emmanuelle, give me a text to copy-edit. Hard copy, if you don't mind. Anything you have, I just need to do some work."

"I've got a fresh-laid novel. Is that OK?"

"Perfect. Please sweep up behind me, I'm a lousy copy-editor, as you know. But I love doing it."

"I always sweep up in any case. The copy is already on my screen."

She slips the pile of paper into a manila envelope. She looks at me with her beautiful eyes full of grammatical rules as she smiles and nods her head sceptically.

"Are you alright?" she asks softly.

I put on a smile for her and wink clumsily while swiping a red felt-tip from her stack. The corridor is quite empty and I stride down it athletically, slip past the receptionist and exit the office. Rain is falling. I put the envelope over my head and scuttle off to the library.

The local library is modern and it still has a writer's name attached to it even though its principal activity is to lend out DVDs. It's been made fairly uncomfortable on purpose to dissuade people from settling down for long stays. It's got more in common with a supermarket than with a place of

bookish contemplation. I like it, it's easy to tame. Despite the wall-high windows, it allows you to feel the silence of books. Most of them are recent and the smell of glue and ink dominate the legendary odour of dust and paper. I find a vacant table between sports and science, where traffic should stay sparse. I put my jacket on the back of a chair to dry it off, I disable my mobile phone, unsheathe the copy, wipe the wet from the front page and switch on my eagle editorial eye. I'm determined to vanquish the epidemic of *er* and *ez* endings that's killing the French past participle, and I shall do battle until evening.

15

The readers' panel meeting is a set-up. Ever since the day I saw a title on our list that had not been approved at a board meeting, I knew the game was over. The readers' panel acts out the drama of decision-making according to an immutable ritual and it makes the bulk of the selections, but if just one title slips through the filter then it isn't a filter any more. A decision to submit an author's work to public scrutiny, though we may make it three hundred times a year, is never an inconsequential act. There are at least ten clear rules that guide our choice of texts: the holy doctrine of the series (to which one-offs serve as an antidote), the rule of the right moment (with its antidote in a multiplicity of book-launch dates), the rule of topicality (with its antidote in the surprise effect), prize strategy (to counter it we have arranged for all the prizes go to a handful of publishers), the rule of there being no money (to counter which we invented money), the rule of the hot genre (to cope with which we invented new and even hotter genres)… and so on. These clear and magnificently flexible criteria help us feel more comfortable when we declare our likes and dislikes, and they also cloak the twenty other hidden rules that actually determine the choices

we make. These murky motivations arise from different tastes, affinities, and cultures: because things resemble what we already like, because they are different, because they make us angry, because we remain faithful to our teenage years or to our teachers—or to friendship and love, which are perfectly respectable reasons for publishing a book. Talent being also perceptible in bed.

I'm in the chair, and I insist on my arms. The others sit in a circle around me on armless chairs. They are characters in a novel we've been writing together for many years. Each plays a more or less involuntary role. I know that giving a text to this or that reader is a way of ditching it. I'm rarely surprised by the outcome of such games. Each reader has his or her favourite domain. Some have a more developed sense of the reading public than others, they have a gift. Others have a feel for newness and experiment. They go for risk and call for patience. Sometimes they turn out to be right in the long term, but they are always wrong in the eyes of the bean counters.

There are large editorial committees composed of distinguished writers who co-opt each other and pick young buds worthy of growing up to join them. They're ponderous and lavish machines well suited to literary fiction and to some kinds of non-fiction. They can turn out to be less than adroit nearer the real heart of publishing, which is to make sure the firm can stay in business. The moment of decision fascinates outsiders to such an extent that many of them think that's all publishers do. But it's only the start of the publisher's real work.

The committee I've built up is a group of professionals who are for the most part readers rather than writers and in addition have a clear idea of all the work that has to be done behind the scenes.

"First we have to decide who's going to deal with the novel that Valentine dropped when she cleared off," Meunier begins aggressively. "I think trusting her was not perhaps the greatest idea since sliced bread."

"I accept that kind comment as intended for me, and I'll deal with the book."

"Wouldn't we have grounds for rejecting it? Her story of tense teens is quite a flimsy thing, isn't it? Who's read it?"

"You mean to say you want to go back on your word after having said yes to a budding novelist?"

"She's not likely to do us much damage."

"Maybe you don't feel the same way, but I would be utterly ashamed…"

"Should I minute this trustful and edifying exchange?" Sabine inquires.

"Definitely! It's important. I shall edit this text myself, and we'll produce a handsome book that will win the prize for first novels, it'll get a mention in the 'New Voices' column in all the weeklies, and it'll get into the bookshops and onto the web at its own pace. Nothing out of the ordinary. Let's talk about the new Balmer. Marc, did you read it?"

"Yes. God knows I love Balmer and I'm always on his side, but I have to say that this one left me feeling let down.

I'm sorry to be disappointed, but honestly, his story of a ship lost in the Arctic pack ice, even if there are some pretty girls on board…"

"Well, I like it," Meunier interrupts unexpectedly. "Don't tell me you didn't laugh at the scenes with the dog. And I think the way it's built like a game of dominos is very appealing. In any case, we're relying on Balmer. At the rate things are going, we'll need him to rescue us pretty soon."

"Notwithstanding, I do prefer his love story or even his short pieces on the raft of the *Medusa*."

"Has anybody else read it?"

"I have," Sabine says, interrupting her note-taking. "But I'm not on the board."

"That doesn't prevent you from giving your opinion…"

"I prefer his love stories because I like love stories, especially the one about the blonde girl in Ireland, but I think his new book is funny and I think it's a good idea to ruffle the reader from time to time."

"Would you publish it?"

"Without the slightest hesitation."

"Marc, is it a no, or a yes but?"

"It's a yes, of course."

I'm glad that exchange didn't require any input from me. The outcome was never in doubt, but I prefer decisions not to come directly from the chair. Balmer is a friend and I think that, come what may, not publishing him would be a serious mistake.

16

Once an author acquires an audience, everyone wants him to write the same book one more time. Readers, traders, the publisher (especially when he claims the contrary)—barely anyone wants him to do anything else, except the author, who may sometimes be reluctant. Publishing a literary opus is quite different from publishing a sequence of books as if they were just pearls on a string. A life's work contains weak moments, mysteries that are only elucidated in the course of time, and stumbles that sometimes turn out to be irredeemable. It can also come to a halt. Despite this, some writers manage to write the same book time and again and nonetheless construct what the French call an *œuvre*.

What can Geneviève want from me this morning? We've not said a word to each other since that indigestible sole. Coming out of the office we turn to the left.

"Where are you taking me?"

"We're obliged to walk a bit, my dear, because Mme Martin has closed down. But I'm sure it's no great burden on your long legs to slog through the neighbourhood with

me. We're even going to pass by your new publisher's place!"

"Can you guess why I want to see you?"

"Let me see. To have the pleasure of paying the lunch bill? If you're in an affectionate frame of mind, to turn the knife in the wound? Maybe to keep an iron in the fire in case you run into trouble one of these days? With glorious long-legged Geneviève, it could be anything! Go on in, it's here."

The bistro is a thoroughly bistro-like bistro equipped with brand new period decor. I presume they concoct the dishes fifty kilometres away and warm them up in a steamer or a wave-oscillation machine...

I take just a bit more time than I need to peruse the menu. I want to taste Geneviève when she's properly marinated. I go for an extended but ascetic meal: tomato salad, cod. To express my mood. She gets it straight away.

"So you're really cross."

"Don't let that stop you from having duck pâté and hare stew."

"Bouzy?"

"Why not a lesser bordeaux? Graves, for instance."

"Is it that bad?"

"In any case, the food is not likely to be good. In which case..."

"Alright, I won't wait until dessert. What I want is for you to read my manuscript."

"The one you've done for Brasset? You're pulling my leg."

"No. I've finished it. They've read it; they're going to set it in print and I can't imagine it appearing without your having read it and telling me what you think of it."

"I don't think anything."

"You can't refuse."

"I don't understand. I've never changed a single word in your writing. I've never picked you up on anything. I've never had you revise so much as a paragraph. I don't recall ever asking you to change the hair colour of your blonde heroines. And yet… You've shown me thirty times that you know how to write a book!"

"I need you to read it. You won't read it when it's been printed, and I can't go around promoting it if you haven't read it."

"I don't need to read it. First, because I know what's in it, and secondly, because I've got to catch up on the latest Proust."

"How's your cod?"

"Guess. I warn you that if you carry on like that I'll make you taste it! Stop crying, you're a big girl now."

"On the contrary, you're making me laugh. Look at my hare…"

She picks up a piece of meat on her fork and holds it out towards me. I eat it.

"Not bad. Would you ever be capable of writing the opposite of what you write? Of coming out of your shell to try something new?"

"I've never really tried."

"Do you think you might be able to think about it?"

"What do you mean, exactly?"

"I'm going to send Sam and Greg to see you. They'll explain."

I think I dropped off at my desk. Hunger wakes me up: hardly surprising after that kind of a lunch. Nothing gets into the system faster than tomatoes and cod. Instant absorption. I'll call Adèle and invite her out to dinner somewhere. She'll know where. Seeing what time it is she must be ferrying fat old Bouchut to the broadcast studio. He'll sell piles of his books once again, he will. If only I knew what I've done with my mobile… Since my desk has been cleared of clutter I can't find anything any more. I must have stuck it under my reader.

There's a light knock at my door. I put on my frozen smile. What comes round the edge is the face of Valentine.

"So there you are! You've finally come to say farewell. I imagine it's not very usual in rock music circles, but in publishing it's still the norm."

"Farewell!"

"Stay! Sit down, and that's an order."

She's wearing trousers without rents and a sweater without stripes and has a big bright yellow comb in her locks.

"So your guitar star is taking you away for good? Have you turned into a roadie?"

"No, not really. He was a bit too much of a star and not enough of a guitar, if you see the kind of guy I mean."

"No, no, I don't see, but it's no trouble imagining. Is the Crécy Bang keeping you on?"

"Nope, again. Rather, I'm not keeping on with them. They did me a good turn so I've no regrets."

"Did you earn a big heap of money?"

"Decent, but they took me to the limit, and I think I'm pretty hooked by books. I wanted to check."

"Which means you're coming back this way?"

"This way, or more precisely to the neck of your wood, if you get my drift."

"I see what you mean very clearly in a general sense. I'm quite relieved because that means that Maud's manuscript ends up in your court. I'd been lumbered with it, surprise, surprise."

"The other reason I came back is that she was so happy when I called her. I kept on thinking about it. I remembered: it was *you* who did the reading."

17

"I've got beer this time."

"No thanks. I'd rather have a drop of wine."

She pulls her skirt down over her knees as if apologizing for it being too short. But there's really no need to conceal her legs.

"Another reason I moved on was because I wanted to see how the lads would manage on their own. They kept on at it. That's good news. They were the ones who invented the name. Do you like it?"

"It's more inspiring than 'Endgame'. No, I mean it's very good, and it's very kind as well."

"We've been working away, but we'll wait until we've got a decent stock. What I'm doing at the moment is looking for proto-electronic authors. I'm scrabbling around finding texts we can take over and set up with reader's guides and video game add-ons. Alphonse Allais, Oulipo, Lewis Carroll. People like that. And we're also working on new things. We're tracking down writers."

"Kind of like the old job, in a way…"

"Yes, and that's why I'd like some answers to my questions."

"I kept your list here, in my drawer. For the most part they don't need any answers. They work perfectly well as questions. You make more headway with questions than with answers."

"All the same…"

"Just one thing: you're worried about not knowing how to spot literature in the manuscripts you read. You're afraid of not being sufficiently cultivated, of not knowing the canon and its principal movements, you're afraid of missing the main point and passing over hidden gems. The worry is inevitable and it won't ever go away. Nothing will ever lay it to rest, because nobody will ever be able to master the whole field as you describe it and that you think a prerequisite for doing your job. What ought to reassure you is that literature's gatekeeper is not you. Nor are the writers themselves. Literature isn't something pre-existing that you insert into a text, it's a very complex construction that's built only with hindsight, and by all. Writers contribute to it, that's for sure, the publisher and the imprint certainly add their mark, but then it's for the media, the booksellers, the academy, and secondary and primary schools to decide. They don't agree with each other, they keep changing their views, and so literature never stops changing its boundaries and shape. Writers you thought had vanished make a comeback, and some you thought set up for eternity disappear. There's a hard core left over that everyone agrees about, but not everyone actually likes them."

"Proust?"

"Proust, Balzac, Goethe, James, Turgenev, Verga, Lowry, Duras… Your teachers cut wafer-thin slices off them and served them up to you dutifully all through your school years. Which doesn't mean they aren't brilliant, by the way. That would be too simple."

"But what can I do to reduce the risk of making a mistake?"

"Read, obviously. Read everything, all the time. And then you have to have strong likes. If you really like the text you're publishing, then it's already taken a step towards the first stage of its afterlife."

She pulls down her skirt unthinkingly, takes a sip of red wine. She has a very individual way of paying attention. I like her blend of simulated naivety and simulated confidence. Unless both are genuine, of course.

"Sometimes it's hard to decide if you really like something."

"It's worth making an effort to find out. That also helps solve another problem you raise: 'How does one say yes?' You've had that experience already, and you know very well that it's not difficult at all. What you need to learn is how to say 'no'. That's a more viable decision, financially speaking. So our job can be boiled down to three thousand 'nos' for one 'yes'. That's enough answers for now. How do you like the côtes du rhône?"

"No idea. It seems soft and red. It goes to your head as well. What's happening at the moment is really exciting. Things are changing. I'm very happy."

"Alright, off you go. I'm hungry and I have to get back to Adèle."

"I'm having dinner with Maud, *my* novelist."

"Bosom pals already?"

"I don't know."

"Is she appealing?"

"I don't know."

She vanishes in a whirl through the open office door, stops on the threshold, and turns round to wave goodbye. I empty my glass to her health. At long last I look at the signatures folder that's been on my desk since the end of the afternoon and quite irrationally I imagine that my own dismissal letter must be inside. I stretch out my hand slowly, hold my breath as if it mattered in the slightest, and raise the board cover like a poker player opening his hand of cards, cast a glance, and guess… They're all rejection letters that Sabine has written for me. "Thank you for sending us your…" "It has many qualities, but…" "Looking forward to reading your next…" I sign them, making a point of writing my name neatly beneath my name. Am I relieved?

"Adèle, I'm hungry."

"The programme is almost over. Are you listening in?"

"Not really. Is your man Bouchut doing alright?"

"He's perfect. As always. He'd have had a huge impact in the days of Pivot."

"I can do without your old flames, thank you very much."

"A missed opportunity, alas. What do you want for dinner? There's nothing in the house."

"I'll eat a whale or a donkey, I don't care. As long as it's not too long coming. Aren't you too shattered?"

"As soon as the programme's finished I'll go to the bathroom, it's a great place for thinking, and I'll call you back with a bright idea. Pack up your briefcase while I'm putting my face on. I'll put some red on my lips and some black around my eyes, and on my hands I'll smear a dollop of cream."

18

I've decided to make this a reading-free weekend. I left my reader switched off in the middle of my desk and didn't take any manuscripts home with me. I want to rest my eyes and daydream methodically. Nor have I brought the list of Robswood's initial plans. I am nobody today and I'm taking my body for a walk along well-trodden paths, like a pet dog on a leash. Sometimes I pull on it to speed up a bit or to get back on track. The countryside looks awfully like countryside, there are leaves on the branches and grass in the fields, a cow underneath an apple tree, the authentic silence of the countryside, a few farm noises and a coating of green boredom spread thick all over the ground. I walk at a steady pace and bend my knees gently at each step in a way I wouldn't dream of exercising in Paris, as I'd be far too scared of being taken for Groucho Marx. I had set out to walk as far as the stream at the bottom of the valley where it makes silver shards sparkle in the long grass, but I don't feel up to it. I'm tempted by the short cut to the village, and I yield to the temptation.

I've put on a dented hat I found hanging on a coat stand in the garage and I would so much like to bump into someone so

I could raise it deferentially, but there isn't anybody around. I can't imagine what anybody would be doing here at this hour. Two or three scattered houses confirm I'm on the right road and that I'm getting nearer to human habitation. There's not a soul to be seen around the houses but you can guess there's heat and light powered by the hardy passions that silently animate the rural bourgeoisie.

The village is empty. Presumably because it's still early. There's just a greengrocer and a cheese seller setting up their market stalls. They go back and forth wordlessly between the square and their vans. I salute them with my hat, they respond with a nod. In the café I stand at the bar to drink an espresso and I resist the temptation of a glass of calvados. The barman is in cahoots with a market trader complaining about the constantly revived and always deferred plan to change market day.

I go over to the baker's to get my own croissant and as I hover I buy a portion of flan as well. I bring them back to eat at the bar. I eat slowly, chewing each mouthful until every bit of taste has been extracted. I peck the very last crumbs. I order another espresso to wash it down. I manage to kill a good ten minutes. The headline in the newspaper lying on the counter mentions flooding and climate change. It also shows a photograph of a pair of *boulistes* who've won a trophy. I think I ought to take up pétanque. It's a reassuring activity because you can always start over, and a stimulating one too, because you can never tell how a throw will turn out. I've already got the hat, all I need is the skill.

The butcher makes it quite clear that he's giving me the silverside as a personal favour, because it's me. He would much prefer to fob me off with one of the rolled roasts stuffed with Emmental and whatnot and decorated with parsley moustaches that he's got lined up like soldiers on parade in his refrigerated display. As he trims my piece he lets out all the village news, which, said twice over, still takes less than five minutes.

As I pass through the village square I take in a bag of Jerusalem artichokes and a fresh-baked baguette.

"Back already!" Adèle says with surprise. "I thought you wanted to have a long walk."

"But I did have a long walk."

"Just don't try asking for lunch at eleven thirty."

After that she says nothing, except, now and again, "Are you going to be under my feet for much longer?" I've peeled the artichokes, which are in the colander, ready for steaming. Adèle is lying on the couch with a pashmina over her shoulders. She's reading. She looks rather well this morning.

I walk around the low table twice with my hands clasped behind my back, make a loop via the kitchen, drink a glass of water, open a bottle of wine, and come to a sudden halt in front of the bookcase. "Hang on," I say to myself, "I'll have a little read." Not for work, mind you, just a little reading to reset myself. If all you read are manuscripts you lose your bearings. The chances of reading a masterpiece are

virtually zero, reading a worthwhile text is more likely, but if you want to be sure a text is good, you have to read it in the company of masters, not just in the company of other decent manuscripts. That way I'll stick to my decision not to read this weekend and to rest my eyes while rejuvenating my vision at the same time. It strikes me as a really good idea. I look through the titles so as to make the right selection. I can feel Adèle smirking behind my back. I'm sure she's put her book down open on her lap and is looking at me with a twisted smile on her lips.

I take Queneau's *L'Instant fatal* and *Bel-Ami* by Maupassant. The two ends of the spectrum. One is inimitable, the other has been imitated too often. Two men from Normandy. One internal vista, one external. Metaphysics and reality. Doubt and certainty. Anxiety in both. I can recite pages from both works, and I'll read them in alternation, a poem, then a chapter, slowly, to make myself as tender as a sunchoke soaked in gravy.

I'll take the half of the sofa that belongs to me. Adèle is pretending to read. I open the two books in my lap, one on top of the other. I just have to slide them this way or that to go from Maupassant to Queneau and back. It's like a mouse click I've invented for myself.

19

"Balmer, atten-tion!"

"Yessir! At your command!"

"So, what's the verdict?"

"I don't understand all of it, but it's great fun. Two good things about it: the youngsters have got a taste for writing, they know what it is, and second, they're into games, which is definitely the shortest path to the reading public."

"You said they're based in writing, but obviously it's not the same kind of…"

"But you wouldn't want it to be the same, you old fogey! If you look more closely, though, it's not so very different. I really like Valentine's idea about proto-electronic authors. It's a great way of rereading hundreds of works, using interactive games and wheezes to get them off the page and into interesting potentialities. To be honest with you, it excites me no end, and I can't be the only one."

"I'll get started on it, then."

"What's your part, exactly? Are you putting in lots of dosh?"

"Nothing significant," I tell him. "Just my life savings. I don't need a partner at the moment. I'm working for them,

not really with them, because I wouldn't know how, but I'm issuing more or less imaginary contracts with quite unlikely people. I give advice when it's asked for… In fact I'm having lots of fun seeing how the taste for writing is passed on."

"What I like about it is that the dynamic comes from the writers and not from the mode of delivery," says Balmer. "Meunier was telling me about his future set-up. He can only see text as it now is and how he's going to stuff it down new media whether it fits or not. Media are expensive things."

"Did you sign the contract?"

"Yes."

"You know the editorial committee had a debate about your text?"

"I'm sure it did. It's not altogether boilerplate. I have a debate about it with myself! I'm a bit worried about it. I wonder how readers will react, whether they'll keep on with me or move away. Frankly, though, I don't see how to change it."

"There's always a way, but nobody's asking you to do that. I'm just saying that if the committee had to talk about it, it may get talked about outside as well. Don't forget you'll need to come and walk the sales reps through it. I think this time you really have to."

"No problem."

"Don't leave without the latest Hautement, hot off the press. And you have to read it!"

*

Meunier is not a happy bunny. He makes this known loud and clear even as he comes into my office. Valentine is back, but re-hiring her is out of the question. The firm is not a carousel, interns are not in charge, an example has to be made. By the way, did you have that word with the interns?

Sabine is in a mood. She collects the signatures folder and puts a fresh one in the same place on my desk. Her face is closed and I don't enjoy the usual benefit of either her smile or her bounce.

"Something wrong, Sabine?"

"No, why should anything be wrong? Everything's fine. The firm is still going, business is booming, there are plans aplenty, and Geneviève's book with Brasset has got a first run of 120,000. Film rights have already been placed with Romain Duris. Everything's hunky-dory. Meanwhile, we're trying to decide whether to re-hire an intern or not!"

"Have you read young Maud's novel?"

"It's not bad, I grant you that. Touching, occasionally funny and sufficiently chick littish to go down well with girls. We'll sell at least 500 copies!"

At times like this I don't argue with Sabine, because she's right and when she's right she's so right that she turns into a kind of unassailable fortress. It's by her doing that I know I have to find a famous writer who doesn't cost too much,

who's been sold in advance, is talented and nice (with Sabine), loyal, productive, timely, who drinks only a little, is modest, amusing, handsome, attentive to personal hygiene and who never drops below 300,000 copies. After all, that's my job.

Adèle is tired and she's staying home today. I can hear her coughing on the phone.

"I'll come and have lunch with you if you like."

"I do like. I also meant to say that I've been thinking this morning and I really intend to meet the Robswood team. After all, I'm the owner of a share in their show and I'd like to get to know them. But please make them realize that I know nothing about what they're doing. I want to appear completely stupid."

"I'll bring you the Hautement that's just out. It's major."

"Do you know how much reading I've got piled up by my bedside? What am I going to say to journalists if I haven't read all those books?"

"You read the flap copy: 'It's a story about a guy…'"

"You're telling *me*?"

"I am. Myself."

20

Sales conferences are rituals that can't be skipped. I've performed at them hundreds of times and, as much as I'm sick to the teeth of book fairs, I still love my sales conferences. They're the first links in the great chain of creative misprision.

I like reps. Brave guys who start up a Peugeot diesel at dawn every day and set off to sell books when they could perfectly well be hitting the road to sell something else, for instance, something that people need and that doesn't have to be explained. Yet they've chosen to sell books, which few people need and that have to be talked up at such length that you end up hardly knowing what you're talking about.

They are optimists, they like books, and they even like the booksellers who don't have enough time for them, moan about the length of the catalogues and groan under the volume of pre-orders and returns. The reps are the pistons in the crazy engine that sells books.

It's nice to see them come to Paris twice a year. They mix accents from north and south, clink beer from Alsace against cider from Brittany, blend champagne with bordeaux. We

feed them, we water them and we anoint them with a jugful of wise words from which they'll retain a sentence, an idea, or a face that they'll pass on to sellers. The dice are cast, they have targets and they know what they're doing, they have a broad idea of how each book will fare, but there's a margin in which they have genuine power. Sometimes they step out of line for a particular title, and then they can become passionate and persuasive. The exception is what writers and publishers come to inspire in them. They trot in and out to recite their book's sacred scripture, its capsule and label: "It's the story of this guy, he meets this girl, but…"

Young Maud quakes with fear. She's vulnerable beneath her simple flower-patterned dress that makes her look as if she's up from the country. She really can't say what she put in the novel she's holding and she can only riffle through the pages, despairing of her ability to make them speak. Valentine sits beside her. She's been hauled back in by Meunier at the last minute (I'll pay for it), but she's not up to helping Maud out. She's her black twin, and mumbles in unison with her.

Looking at them closely and noticing the way they've transformed the reps' postprandial indifference into paternal amusement, I reckon they're scoring. Like Modiano, the jumbo mumbler, only young and female. I put an end to their suffering and let them go into the wings to bewail their incompetence and the death foretold of their offspring, while the reps smile and have a look at the book. The girl's photo is on the back panel. The two of them totter away.

Balmer is an old trooper. I introduce him out of protocol, but everyone knows who he is. He's done a dozen book tours around the country and he knows most of the reps by their first names.

"Are you new to the job? Which region do you do?"

"I've taken over from Thierry, in Brittany."

"Say hi to Kermarec from me."

"Sure will."

Balmer speaks plainly, confidently. He doesn't do a great writer act. He says he's got the willies about this book. He says a few things about it but doesn't go on too long.

"I know you're snowed under, but if you have a chance to look at it, I'd be glad to know what you think. Shoot me an email."

"Do you expect to come to Lyon? *Passages* would be glad to have a signing session."

"If the book takes off, I'm not saying no. Right, Robert?"

"If you think it's worthwhile, of course he'll come down."

When he vanishes behind the black drape and Hautement strides on in his place, it's a different world. Hautement is almost as stratospheric as his name suggests. He is well on his way to the Académie française. He's impeccable, clear, and professional to a tee. He gives a synopsis of his book, lays out his aims, turns them into selling points, situates the book in the sequence of his other books, mentions how

well each of them did and confides his hopes, which sound transparently like sales targets. I've done my job, gentlemen. Now you do yours.

I almost have to come in after him with a few words to make it all sound more human, and especially to stress that the book really is good, and a great deal more anguished than the author let show.

Now it's Meunier's turn to introduce his authors and to announce the winner of the half-yearly sales prize—a week's vacation in Crete. Tonight's get-together will be at the Crazy Horse Saloon. All in a day's work for a real publisher.

"I'm really sorry, we were utterly useless. When I saw she was starting to panic, I got into a nervous state as well and couldn't get a word out. Not that I can manage a great deal at the best of times. But we'd rehearsed it properly, we really had. We spent all morning at it. I made up questions and she learned the answers by heart, but when we saw them sitting there looking at us with their minds mostly elsewhere... they looked enormous and not well disposed."

"Be careful, sales reps have got thick skins! Please don't start crying again. You'll learn, and Maud will too. It's true you didn't put on a great show. You'd have had to be clairvoyant to guess what the book was about. But sometimes those guys do read a thing or two!"

"I'm ashamed. It was my job to calm her down and speak up on her behalf, but my mind was a blank. I messed it up."

"It would perhaps be more accurate to say that your sales pitch technique falls some way short of target."

She dabs her eyes and gives me a broad smile. She shuts my office door gently behind her with the tips of her fingers.

*

"I've also got some good news."

"Really good news?"

"Yes, really good. Le Clézio is going to give us a sirandane a day for an iPhone app. You get the solution the next day."

"Jean-Marie Le Clézio?"

"Yes, Le Clézio, the good-looking guy who won the Nobel Prize. The fair Mauritian."

"How ever did you get Le Clézio?"

"I asked him to meet me, he came, and I told him what I wanted. He thought for a moment. He said yes, and asked me where I came from."

"Catch a falling star…"

"He's very nice."

"You may not be up to snuff with sales reps yet, but you seem to be on a roll as far as writers are concerned."

"I told him you would call. Is that alright?"

"Obviously. How could it not be?"

She's happy with her scoop. It makes her forget to pull down her skirt. You could almost believe she's grown taller. She's looking straight at me and her whole being is full of laughter.

"And what exactly are you planning to get him to do?"

"Sirandanes. They're traditional riddles that old folk set children in our part of the world. Le Clézio collects them. I'm sure he makes some of them up as they're too good to be true. I'll give you an example: 'My maker sells me, my

buyer doesn't use me, and my user doesn't know he has me. What am I?'"

"?"

"A coffin! The idea is to get him to write a few lines of intro, followed by the riddle. The next day we give the solution and set a new puzzle. Plus a few Malagasy designs, like the embroidery you get on ethnic napkins sold to tourists, plus his photo as eye candy for the girls, and that makes a really nice little app. Readers subscribe to the feed and get a fresh dose every morning."

"Will you charge a lot?"

"No, just a few euros. But there'll be lots of subscribers. We're wondering whether to give the riddles in Creole as well, with a translation. Do you think we should?"

"What does that sound like?"

"*Mo zet li anler, li tonm anba; mo zet li anba, li mont anler.* I throw it up and it goes down, I throw it down and it goes up…"

"?"

"A bouncy! A rubber ball!"

"That's even better. You have a wonderful accent. Of course you have to put in the Creole. You'd be making it into two riddles for the price of one. Riddle me ree, perhaps you can tell what my riddle may be…"

"I'm glad."

"So you should be."

"I'd like a drink."

"Red wine."

*

I open my secret closet, take my time to choose, and grant us a pommard 2005 that's certainly not available on any island in the Indian Ocean. I open it with just the tip of the corkscrew. I pour it with care and caution, and we taste it. You could make a meal of a wine like that.

"We saw Geneviève, the Geneviève you mentioned! She said you'd told her to give us a call."

"I put it to her, as a suggestion."

"Well, she didn't get it at all. Not a clue. Sam tried to explain, but he's a bag of nerves and so obsessive about it all that he put her off. I went over it all a second time slowly, but I still had the feeling she didn't understand where we were going—maybe that's nowhere, of course! I'd read all her books before she came and thought they were all terrific, so I told her so. I managed to explain things better by talking about her writing. I don't think she grasped all of it, but I think she'll give us a blog in her own style. A thousand characters and spaces a day with a surprise every time."

"At the rate you're going it'll just bounce along."

"Like a rubber ball! I'd like some more of that wine of yours, it's so rich and velvety it tastes almost like cream."

22

The doctor reckoned Adèle would do herself a spot of good by taking three days' rest. As she finds tearooms to be places of rest, she chose sun-drenched London. She says it's a place where she can plonk herself down without feeling obliged to rush around or do anything in particular, and that the hustle and bustle of London life isn't catching, for her at least. Another advantage is that it is really other whilst being not far away at all. The highly speedy train that takes you there is comfortingly yellow.

That's why she's curled up in a capacious armchair facing me in a flocked and fluffy South Kensington hotel. Tile patterns do mortal combat with flowers, the carpet is drowning under layers of rugs, and curtains over curtains create an atmosphere of snow. A painting over the bed shows a fox hunt, with red-jacketed riders jumping horses over five-barred gates. Adèle is tired, she's resting her head on a cushion in the armchair with her eyes closed. Her shoulders are swaddled in shawls, and I know she's working hard at creating heat.

I am waging merciless war on the remote control in search of BBC World News with mute on. The visuals are quite sufficient, usually.

In her semi-sleep Adèle arranges to meet me at five at a top-notch tearoom she's fond of, near the posh hotels on Piccadilly. It's her not so subtle way of telling me to go away and leave her alone in the meantime. She doesn't need to say it twice. I put on my raincoat and stuff my reader in my pocket before plodding noiselessly down the thick wool pile of the hotel corridor.

It's hard to believe the London Underground isn't suffering from depression, because it plunges deep into the city's dark belly and scurries along narrow tubes scarcely big enough for trains to get into. You dip your head instinctively so as not to bump the ceiling. It's full of mini-skirted girls in high heels and beehive hairdos yapping away under the indifferent eyes of hatted Englishmen and turbaned Sikhs. I'm scanning the *Guardian* on my tablet and the girl sitting next to me reads along with me, with such a casual air of innocence that it makes me smile. I ask her if she's finished the page so I can scroll down. She's offended.

My street in London is Charing Cross Road. One after another bookshops are closing all over town, methodically, faster than the pubs, and the book scene overall is catastrophic. Except on Charing Cross Road. Bookshops there are part of the masonry, they inhere in the very walls. Antiquarian books, porn dives, worn rock albums, Chinese medicine, a bookshop that does nothing but Conan Doyle with Sir Arthur himself in the window. I greet him with a nod as I go by, and think that if I ever smoke a pipe it will be one like Sherlock Holmes's, a fine-looking pipe that provides

both the pleasure of a smoke and the illusion of playing the saxophone. My aim is to get to Number 100, Charing Cross Road. To do so I have to plough a sinuous path through the milling crowd while avoiding the box-office queues, keeping a safe distance from the rickshaw tricycles taking tourists up towards Regent's Park, and stopping myself from stopping to read the sandwich boards (there are none of those left in Paris any more) puffing the latest West End musicals.

Number 100 is the address of a very large and rather sad bookstore with grey-blue flooring and scattered tables with general books, business books, books for young readers (not well displayed), royals, chick lit, gothic horror, spy thrillers, and, near the checkout desk, a pile of a little red funny book detailing Her Majesty's reading habits, a pyramid of American blockbusters, no modern French literature (or a mere sprinkling) and no hoppers of graphic novels (that craze hasn't yet got to these shores)… And right in the middle, there it is: *Die Maschine*. It's the only reason for my coming to this gloomy place that could easily cast you into a slough of despond. The machine is called POD. It looks like a cross between a small combine harvester and a large photocopier. POD stands for Print On Demand. Apparently you just have to wish for a book really hard and POD will make it for you on the spot, like a Japanese chef slicing sushi as you watch.

I proudly hand my reader to the operator and point to a title on my virtual bookshelf. It's a secret copy of a

book that's become unobtainable in print. Evidently the reader can also serve as the cemetery where books will come together at the grand finale, after the great levelling and evening.

23

It's *Ageing in Beijing* by dear old Jacques Bens, a slim volume so perfectly gloomy that it verges on the hilarious, so perfectly passionate that it verges on the aggressive, and so perfectly written that it's just beautiful. I want it to be a surprise for Adèle when we meet for our glass of sherry.

You can't hear paper crinkling through rollers and there's not even a hidden cable connection, but despite this my text just slips into the machine, which then goes into action and prints it off in an entirely smoke-free and oil-free operation. In a single pass it glue-binds the pages and graces them with a cover that may not be a work of art but which at least looks like a book cover. The paper has a slightly dubious feel, being stiff at the fold, but there's no denying POD's achievement: it's allowed me to obtain an unobtainable book.

I reciprocate by making a reasonable contribution and dive back into the swirling throng to forge my way along Piccadilly to the lounge of the Ritz. Oh my Baudelaire! This is the ugly face of *luxe, calme et volupté*. Adèle has chosen a seat at a low table directly underneath a crystal chandelier; her shoulders are hunched as if she were permanently chilly. She's picking at a slice of cucumber perched on a tiny wafer

of buttered sponge that's going to cost me £50. I know she enjoys watching little old English ladies getting pickled on port and guzzling cream cakes. It's a hobby of hers.

I sit down opposite and, doing my best to look as impish as I can, I hand her the Bens. She glances at it.

"Well, well, what a surprise! You had to come all the way to London to find it? You've been going on about it for ages…"

"It's tailor-made, my dearest, just like a suit from Savile Row. An *unicum* just for you. Your own unique and personal copy."

"How come?"

I explain the glorious workings of wonderful POD as I sip a glass of sherry, a drink it would never occur to me to savour in Paris, but which seems self-evident here. I order a second glass on the trot to wash down the tiny canapés among which I have just espied a shrimp bedded in potentially mouth-watering pink mayonnaise. The very special perfume of the smoked black tea called Lapsang Souchong that Adèle is drinking blends in well with the taste of my sherry.

My wife has plans for the day. She wants to have a pint in a pub at peak time (are there any other times?), see a musical and finish off with dinner at Red Fort, that Indian restaurant, don't you recall, where you get delicate dishes fit for a maharajah…

"…or a maharani. Wish granted."

"Any idea for a show?"

"I'm easy. Don't mind seeing anything. *Chicago, Mamma Mia!, Avenue Q, Jersey Boys,* anything but *Les Misérables* because they left Victor Hugo's name off the publicity."

"It's Luc Plamondon's version, you grumpy ignoramus!"

"You should have a bite of this custard tart, it's really glorious. You need to keep going until the curry bell tolls for thee."

I've set aside tomorrow morning for what I consider to be the finest bookshop in Europe: Mr James Daunt's establishment in Marylebone. It's got a modest exterior but inside it turns into a labyrinth. You go from room to room and pass from one section to another. Nothing but dark wood, stairs, gangways and books—all as English as its leather armchairs. Adèle is daydreaming in the long room on the lower floor that constitutes the travel section. Daunt is a courteous host and takes me on an owner's tour, explaining the book-shifting rules he's worked out for his shop, so that what at first appears delightfully haphazard turns out to be the mask of a quite meticulous book traffic scheme, like the re-stocking system that he designed himself. He shows me how it works on a computer near the checkout desk.

Adèle abandons me to go window-shopping in Marylebone High Street. She gives me a hug as she slips out behind my back.

Next to the new releases there's a very prominent table of contemporary classics: Boyd, Coe, Zadie Smith, Monica Ali, Adam Thirlwell, and also Carver, Paul Auster and Brautigan

from the other side of the Atlantic. As well as Tarun Tejpal, Vikram Seth and Aravind Adiga from other parts of the English-speaking world.

"The turnover on this table is quite incredible. It's the only one like it. My bookshops are just about the last of their kind left in London. We don't discount, we don't do three-for-two, we don't indulge in marketing gimmicks, we just sell books. Customers like it that way."

"Why do you have so few French books?"

"Because they're not read."

24

"If people don't read French books, perhaps that's because there aren't any on offer."

"Maybe, but that's an issue for publishers, whose ranks I have no wish to join."

I exit and go to meet Adèle in a shoe shop. She's sitting on a pouf with a strange blue object on her right foot: a kind of high-heeled boot with glitter-dust spangles. She's obviously not quite made up her mind about the footwear.

"Do you really think I'll go for them? Wearing them wouldn't be an issue if I were living in London. But I wonder if I would want to in Paris."

"You can buy them in order to resolve the issue. If you end up not wearing them in Paris, then we'll come back so you can wear them here."

She's tired, tired and happy, but as soon as we settle down in the train from St Pancras I can feel work worries tugging away at her mind. She wants my reader so she can catch up on a book she has to praise to the skies tomorrow at lunch with a literary critic. But she doesn't feel like reading. The

reader is switched on in her lap but her eyes are staring into the far distance, towards the dark night of the chunnel.

I must have made a huge faux pas because they're all on top of me the moment I get into the office with an armful of books from England. Meunier, Sabine and Emmanuelle, all looking harried and dismayed. I put down my load and smile.

"What came over you?" Meunier asks.

"What do you mean? When? Where? I've just come back from London…"

"Don't try telling me you've forgotten! Ginette Perrault is hopping mad. She considers herself insulted, manhandled and humiliated, and she's got a point! She's even threatening to cancel publication, how about that! And I can't say I blame her!"

"What's wrong with her book?"

"Have you seen how you edited it?"

"I have to admit it's my fault as well, to some extent," Emmanuelle interrupts. "I was overloaded, as usual, and I didn't do a proper check. I just had a glance and then trusted you because you're a very good copy-editor, despite what you say, but this time I must say you really went too far."

"I don't recall. I just corrected spellings—*driving on the write*, that sort of thing."

"So may I inquire, for instance, why you changed the heroine's name?"

"But 'Lisette' isn't a real name! Don't you think 'Simone' sounds better? Is that all she's making a fuss about?"

"And why did you cut a whole scene in the garden, just after the shouting match?"

"That scene would have been better if it had never been thought of. Did you read it?"

"May I remind you that we accepted the manuscript and committed ourselves to turning it into a book—not into a different book! Why did you change the colour of the dress? How do you account for it being yellow instead of green? What right do you have? You've never done anything like this before. Are you going bananas?"

"It was a horrid shade of green."

"What's even worse is that you introduced scenes of your own, in your own handwriting, in red pencil, in the work of one of our authors. Comical scenes, moreover. 'Then Simone, who wasn't particular about these kinds of things, decided to get laid, and aimed straight for the flies of the headmaster who couldn't help blushing or holding back an erection that suddenly illuminated the staff room.' In a novel by Ginette Perrault! Then further on: '"Fuck me!" yelled the well-brought-up young lady. "Bugger the local yokels and their backwoods, I'm off to town to put myself about and buy an outfit that'll excite louche women in black tuxes."' In a novel of provincial life!"

"Did I really insert that passage? Funny thing, it doesn't strike me as well written."

And that's when I recollect exactly the rainy afternoon that I spent in the public library. My jacket was wet and was taking

a long time to dry out on the back of my seat. I remember that as the sun went down I got tired of hunting for spelling mistakes and wondered what would happen to texts when anyone could get them on their readers and alter them as they pleased—turning Proust's madeleine into a shortbread cookie, sprinkling perfume on the red lady, getting up Pauline Réage's skirt, cheering up a novel by Bernanos with a few side-splitting gags, inventing this or that, turning round a couple of sentences, or calling Madame Bovary Adèle to please someone's wife. I'm sure I intended to rub it all out and then I forgot. Alas, I am a too modern man. I am far ahead of my times. I'm misunderstood, and I therefore think it is prudent for me to beg for pardon by admitting that I made a great big mistake.

25

"I don't know what got into me. I must have had my mind on something else. I let myself go."

"If you want to write, go ahead, we'll sign you up…"

"What did Ginette say?"

"She was screaming mad to begin with, you know what she's like, then I calmed her down and agreed to have Emmanuelle go over it with her from top to bottom. Not exactly a time saving method, and I don't have to tell you that time is…"

"There's one thing that's awkward," Emmanuelle butts in. "When she got over the upset and we got down to work on the text, she decided she wanted to keep some of the changes. They set off new ideas. She'd like to know if that would be OK with you. Especially the funny bits."

"Of course it's OK. Not a problem."

"The outstanding problem is that Meunier insisted we had to erase everything and delete all trace of your work. She was worried that we'd take out too much."

"I'll take her out to lunch. As an initial bid for forgiveness we'll give her a handsome jacket in colour."

"What do you mean by a handsome jacket?"

"Whatever appeals to her."

As soon as they're gone I switch on my reader to read the newspapers. I've perfected the ultimate reading position: heels crossed on desk, tablet at exactly the right distance down my leg to suit my spectacles, slightly against the light, and the swing chair reclining. I'll begin with *L'Équipe* for the sports, then go on to *Le Monde*, *Le Figaro* and *Libération*, steering clear of the book pages. I stopped reading those ages ago. At the time when Adèle was tearing her hair out and exploding in anger every week: "Just look at the mess they're making! How am I supposed to do my job if *Le Monde* only ever talks about dead writers, *Libération* only features foreign writers, and *Le Figaro* sticks to the mummies in the Académie française? What are we supposed to do about our budding French writers?" Being a book publicist is a tough assignment. Apparently things have improved since then, but I haven't gone back to the book pages. The girls in the office give me cuttings when our own authors get any notices. I read those, but I don't want to know what else was on the page. I must remember to read *Publishers' Weekly* as well, not just for the job ads. I am very fond of the "Book Deals" column, listing all the dismal titles that have been acquired. I amuse myself by imagining the books they misrepresent. I must also read the feature on digital rights, an issue that nourishes Meunier's nocturnal anxieties. He's sure that publishers could well lose their shirts over it. He loves putting himself into a tizzy.

Emmanuelle turns up, enters with a conspiratorial air, and closes the door behind her.

"I just wanted to say that I laughed out loud. Actually, I did reread the whole thing, but your insertions were so funny that I left them in to see what would happen. And we saw. I'm sorry."

"Mme Ginette Perrault isn't exactly a whole heap of fun!"

"Meunier poured oil on the waters, all the same."

"Do you think she really would leave us?"

"Not a chance. She's truly delighted with all the hoo-ha. It makes her feel that her publisher is at last looking after her on a full time basis."

"Any idea where I could take her out for lunch?"

"Off the top of my head, I'd say a dainty tea-and-sandwich place with flower-painted porcelain tableware and embroidered napkins."

"What a prospect! Double jeopardy! Find me an address, I don't go to places like that."

"Above all, you must remember not to order breakfast blend at luncheon. That would be a really serious mistake."

26

In the meantime the youngsters have sat Adèle down in the middle of the sofa. They've placed a pair of readers and two smartphones in her lap. Sam and Valentine are on either side. Gregor and Kevin are leaning over the back, and Monkey, Kevin's geeky younger brother, flutters around the group like an imp or genie.

"Are you really called Monkey?"

"Of course not, it's only what idiots call me. They say it's the name of a character in an old manga, and I look like him."

"As long as it's only the looks you share!"

"I have the same wristband as well."

"Beer for all and wine for Valentine!"

"Not for me, I'm too young and I don't drink alcohol. Can I have a Coke?"

They switch on the devices and start the demo, pointing fingers at screens.

"First off, we've got some simple items, but they work well because people find them familiar. Poem of the day, thought

of the day, proverb of the day, the rhyming horoscope that Grangaud's providing us with, and polemical squibs poking fun at things. All written in decent French prose."

"Do you always add artwork?"

"Yes, at least as a background at the start. Animation will come later."

"Are you the ones who choose the poems?"

"Yes, with the help of some friends. We actually get the best results with the poems. Loads of people who would never open a book of poetry really enjoy reading a poem a day."

"Mind you, we go for the tops: Apollinaire, Ashbery, Roubaud, Ludovic Janvier, last week it was Follain. We're going to do Jouet next."

"We've also got Today's Short Story. Extremely short. We'll be putting up Fénéon's three-liners soon. People like true stories. They'll be a real hit."

"Here are the sirandanes."

"The line-drawings are lovely."

"They're embroidery patterns from Madagascar. Want to try?"

"I'll have a go."

"There you go. On the home page there's a sirandane in Creole: 'Dilo dibou, dilo pendan'. If you can't understand it, tap the screen once and the translation comes up: 'Water standing, water falling'. If you don't get the solution right away, wait a day and you get: 'Kan, coco'. One tap, and there it is in French: 'Sugar cane, coconut'."

"That's adorable. Can I try another one?"

I'm in the kitchen, with my ears open. Adèle's reactions are what I'm interested in, and I keep listening for them as I make dinner. I've given the French fries another turn in the oven before putting them back in the deep-fat fryer to have them come out crisp and crunchy. I make French fries once in a blue moon, yet I always get stressed about having them turn out just right. What I'm making today are Tournedos Rossini. Just for fun but also to express solidarity with the food culture of my young colleagues, I bought whole-grain round bread buns from the baker's and I'm going to serve the steak inside them just like "beef patties in the Hamburg style", as early translators of American crime fiction used to say whenever someone tucked into a hamburger.

"We're also developing reading tools. The idea is to exploit the technology to make people read in a new way, or rather, to reread in a new way."

"How so?"

"We make the lines of the poem come up one by one, at our own speed and in whatever order we like. Sam, who has a sentimental soul, puts in a musical backing."

"Don't you make fun of me, Kaffir girl!"

"Shut up, racist scum!"

"Kevin's put up Queneau's *Story as You Like It*. Click on your option, and up pops the next line. Do you want to

know what happened to the peas, or what happened to the beanpole?"

"Can I have a go?"

Meanwhile, speaking of myself,

27

I am slowly adding one spoonful of balsamic vinegar to three of olive oil and stirring absent-mindedly as I keep my ears trained on the conversation.

It's Kevin's turn to kick off.

"Monkey has done something really hot, I have to say. He's written an S+7 engine."

"A what?"

"You type in a text, and the algorithm replaces each noun with the seventh noun following in the dictionary. It's funny, and it's mechanical. It puts a happy smile on commuters' faces. Gregor's also doing a heap of easier stuff to help people produce their own writing: *bouts rimés* generators, where all you have to do is write the beginning of the verse, acrostic generators, hidden-letter programs, and refrain machines to manufacture song lyrics…"

"I'll never have time to try them all."

"Maybe not, but you'll have time to choose the one you want to try. You mustn't miss Miss Valentine's Institute for Prosthetic Literature."

"I've used schoolbook classics, the program allows you to

make all kinds of modifications, such as changing characters' clothes, giving them new names, or swapping their genders."

"Is it an attempt to improve the classics?"

"Not really, not always, but it's entertaining. We're experimenting."

In the depths of my kitchen, I'm vaguely reminded of something or other, but I choose to concentrate on cooking the wafer biscuits that are to go with the fruit salad. I'm ashamed.

Balmer arrives behind schedule, as usual.

"I'm sorry, I had my ear bent by the owner of a small bookshop who kept asking what would become of him. How far have you got? What are you up to, Adèle?"

"I'm reading and playing."

"Which?"

"Both, officer, sir."

"Since Balmer's here, I'll let you look at the stuff we've not put up yet."

"Well, those are really minor," Monkey declares. "I'm dropping out and going to help the big chef in the kitchen."

"This is nearer to traditional reading. Every morning Balmer writes a comical pen-portrait of the *Mona Lisa*. When he's had enough of that, he'll move on to the complete works of Philippe de Champaigne…"

"We've also got Geneviève's 1,000-character column!"

"Her column is just fantastic. I go crazy waiting for the

next instalment every day. She turns it in in the middle of the night and Kevin gets it online before dawn."

"Listen, what's brilliant is that she had us over to her place for a party, and it was like, wild. Sam couldn't get over it. So he stayed over!"

"Are you getting jealous?"

I'm not remotely surprised but the info is too entertaining for me not to poke my head out of the kitchen.

"Good old Geneviève is still in top form, I see! By the way, her piece, I didn't get it, this morning."

"No, because we're adding the English version. From tomorrow you can click on a Union Jack and go straight to the English."

"You have overnight translators?"

"Yes, that's easy. We'd quite like to have a version in an impossible language as well, just for fun. But we can't agree on which one. I want Finno-Ugric, but Valentine wants Chuvash."

"I like the poetry of Gennady Aigui."

"I'm planning something with Mr Balmer," says Monkey. "He's going to write texts that can be re-arranged. You'll be able to move chunks around on screen and get a different story. What's difficult is that I don't want horizontal sections, like in guess-who-I-am games, I want diagonal permutations. Mr Balmer is struggling with it and way behind schedule, but I'm not criticizing him because it will be really nice and he'll write things as sad as epics that are going to make everybody cry, once they've been read."

28

Adèle is glad to stretch a leg.

"I'm stiff all over and my head's bursting. I think I deserve a glass of wine."
    "This is a bottle of morgon."
    "Guten morgon?"
    "It had better be! Dinner time!"

They're hungry, and hunger is just about the only thing that can shut them up for a moment. They clap when I bring in the fries, then fall into devout silence to taste them. They're burning hot, crisp outside, soft inside, and slightly disturbing, because they're not evenly cut and don't come from the freezer. Are they OK, nonetheless? Was that an unambiguous OK? They're delicious? Oof, I passed the test. Now I have to gird myself for a silent duel with Monkey. He stares at me and I stare back. Will he, won't he? He's still not sure. He looks at me and nods. I concede the match.

    "Yes, I've got some."

*

So I go to the kitchen to get the ketchup I've made for him. He smiles from ear to ear. I've become his ally. He carefully lays his piece of beef filet and foie gras between the two halves of a bun he's buttered with ketchup, and takes a big bite. The meat is tender and yields to the tooth as easily as ground beef.

"Your Big Bob is great," he declares between mouthfuls.

The motion is approved even by the ones who are using forks. Balmer, who inclines towards dinner parties in general and towards this one in particular, tells the story of the time when he invited friends over for a meal. It was to be a leg of lamb, from the freezer. At the last minute his oven broke down, so the lamb stayed as ice-bound as his spuds, and the party had to make do with ketchup on untoasted bread. The youngsters find it funny, but I know the story, because I was one of the guests.

Adèle tells them she's really glad to have had the demo, and it was very nice of them to come and show her the full catalogue of Robswood Publishing. Kevin explains that he and his kid brother have hacked into other publishers' sites to find out what they were up to, so as to have a comprehensive view of the state of the art.

"One thing's clear," Monkey says. "There are three heavyweight software guys working for Éditions Dubois. They're not going to get anywhere fast…"

"Tell me something, Monkey," says Adèle. "I'm not going to do the granny act and ask you what you want to be when you grow up, because you're grown up already and you are what you want to be. But what I'd like to know is how you see yourself a few years down the road."

"You mean after we've sold Robswood to a major for a heap of money? What I'd really like is to play the part of a twenty-five-year-old billionaire who walks down the street in old jeans, a soggy sweater and a baseball cap…"

"No, no baseball cap!" Valentine shouts.

"… without a baseball cap, then, waiting for a good idea to alight on my shoulder. Just imagine: we're all rich, I've got a big wad of money in the bank, I pretend not to care a hoot about it, and I wander round the planet wherever the whim takes me (in global first, if you don't mind!), never knowing exactly where I am. One day I'm sighted in Palo Alto putting a bomb under Oracle, then at Apple HQ in Cupertino, I've also been spotted in Dubai, and I may have been in disguise but that was me coming out of IBM… and I just saunter along with my hands behind my back and my head in the clouds looking for the next big thing to make me another billion. Wouldn't that be the coolest? It's the new frontier! They'll make a movie of my life."

"Well, well," Balmer says. "That is a rather new way of conceiving the life of a publisher."

29

I'm aware of a "depression plot" beaming its microwaves at me. My colleagues have come to the collective decision that I am suffering a serious downer. They whisper about me at the coffee dispenser and handle me like an egg. It's been decreed that I'm liable to crack. It'll be a hairline at the start, then a fracture, then my gooey brain will trickle into the gutter chased down by the yolk of my happier self. That is how my long journey down the dark alleys of the city of shadows will commence.

In fact I'm rather well, but I confess I'm making no great effort to spread the news; that's why the beams are thickening around me. Everyone wants to be my airbag, but their worries are as good as a crown of thorns. People ask me if I slept well. They bring me a piece of chocolate on the grounds that it "cheers you up". They mention as if by chance a benzodiazepate that cardio-relaxes you like nothing else. They offer to reduce my reading load (presumably because they reckon I'm not as sharp as I used to be). I get invitations to children's tea parties, probably to act the clown. They want to send me off to the Jaipur Book Fair. People I wouldn't have a meal with at any price ask me out to their favourite rough bars.

*

"Just have a taste of that Louise Bonne pear!" the head of production tells me, for he owns a garden.

The ideal thing, I am told by depression cognoscenti who seize the opportunity to recite the stages of their own journey to the end of night, would be to "clear my head". The phrase puzzles me: first, because I am attached to much of what is in my head and would not wish to exchange it for a supposedly healthier alternative; secondly, because the unpleasant part of what's in my head causes a number of awkward feelings that are effective intellectual stimulants. So I would not want to clear that out either.

For most people "clearing your head" consists in "taking a long vacation in the sun". Now everybody knows that vacation turns tiger into lamb and sheep into wolf, necessarily tanned of course, and therefore undepressed. What better means of clearing your head can there be than a life on a beach?

It so happens that beaches affect me like a pump. The combined action of sand and sea siphons off my coloured ideas and conducts them over the horizon, leaving only dark thoughts to tan the inside of my skull. It's a perfect way of lowering my spirits, a foolish action that could easily drive me to despair.

I therefore let the waves wash over me and exhibit polite irritation with the syrupy kindnesses of all and sundry. Which ends up convincing every one of them that I really am in a depression. So they serve me another tablespoonful.

Meunier, who tends to keep his distance, plays a technical game, but under the pressure of public opinion he finally makes up his mind to have a word with me:

"You know, if you need a break, it's not a problem, we can cope. You could take Adèle on a trip, or even stay in Paris if you prefer, as you might. You can keep on working from home and stay in touch… Nothing can go wrong…"

"You won't even be able to screw me if my back is turned."

"No need, you're screwed already."

"So what you're saying is that I'm no longer any use."

"Goodness gracious, Gaston! I never said that!"

"But you thought it very loud."

"Not at all. You know you're named after a very fine publishing house and that authors, even Ginette Perrault, in spite of my efforts to the contrary, trust you completely. At least for the time being. Until this evening."

30

A winter has gone by, spring is on its way, yet my mood is autumnal. Robswood is raking it in. Contrary to expectations, Maud's debut novel is a real hit. Old-style publishing is made of surprises. It's not just a critical success, it's a real one. It has ripened from day to day, and has now reached maturity. People want to read the book, they talk about it, lend it to each other, wallow in it and argue about it. We're selling a thousand copies a day. Initial reviews were sweet and short, but now the press is treating the book as a phenomenon to be analysed as it leans over backwards to lure back some of Maud's audience. Her photo is everywhere. Her book has made someone of her. She's a new person: dressed by newly fashionable couturiers and -ières, beheeled and bejewelled, she has acquired poise. Blessed by the god of worried writers, she's not stopped being a nice person and secretly herself. She often appears on TV to give her opinion on topics about which she knows precisely nothing. She does so graciously, gets a plug for her book, and in the studio audience you can make out the shape of her avatar, Valentine. The two of them travel the length and breadth of the country, from bookshops to

regional TV studios. I get notices of her appearances in Metz, Strasbourg, Montpellier, Bordeaux, Rouen, Annecy, Marseille… They're learning the lie of the land, and how to dine out in small towns.

In Paris, meanwhile, Hautement is unenthusiastic about Maud's success, he thinks it was at the expense of what his own book aspired to. In his view the firm is now entirely at Maud's service and has dropped its other writers into a dark hole. We'll have to keep a close watch on him in the coming months to stop him running off to find a better path to glory. Balmer is nonplussed, and he's wondering what he should write next in order to have his own sip of nectar. Valentine's lack of experience apparently allows her to take the rocket-ride as a normal event; after all, hadn't she liked the book first, before anyone else?

"I've just seen Meunier. He's offered me a fixed-term contract. He thinks I've got a good feel for books and wants to 'give me a break'."

"That's the least he could do."

"But I'm really not sure if I should accept. What with Robswood Publishing as well I'd have a lot of work, a lot going on."

"No, you wouldn't, Valentine. You've got one foot in old-style publishing—and what a foot it is!—and the other in the new! You're in just the right position—on the cusp. At the pressure point. Literary publishing has never been in crisis because literary publishing *is* a crisis. That's its

nature. Anyway, you don't say no to Meunier, especially if he's paying you properly."

"Since he's been wooing me he's offering me the moon. By the way, on the same topic, I meant to tell you that Gregor is dropping out of Robswood. Because of me."

"You had a row?"

"No, but he wants to be my boyfriend and I don't want to be his girlfriend. He doesn't want to be near me. He says it hurts."

"That won't be the last time…"

"You think I should say yes because he's a nice guy?"

"Don't be crazy, I never said any such thing. Sort it out yourself."

"You know what? Geneviève is firing on all four and coming up with incredible stories. People can't get enough! Tomorrow's instalment, you'll see, is about a woman with a weight issue who gets her exercise by having her daughter hide chocolate eclairs, muffins and rum babas all over the house! As well as puff pastries filled with cream!"

31

I was reading a typescript on the antiquity of French versification when some person burst into my office. In his fat hand he was holding a reader just like mine.

"Good morning," he said. "Here's your new reader."

"I prefer the old one," I bristled in response. "It's full of truly excellent writing. With lesser literature besides."

"I'll transfer all of it into the new one."

"It works fine, and I would prefer to hang on to it."

"You can't do that, we're changing the whole fleet."

"What 'fleet'?"

"We've now got everyone on board, and as you'll see, the upgrade is much better. It's faster."

"But I read at *my* speed, not the device's. Anyway, the old one is new, and you should never throw away a new thing, especially if it's stuffed with old books…"

"You'll see, screen definition is much sharper, and you can get onto the internet in a split second."

"Split seconds don't register on my biological clock."

"Please be reasonable and hand over your old reader."

"Me and my reader have hardly got to know each

other properly. What's more, I'm not sure I know how to use it yet."

"I'll transfer the entire content into the new one for you."

I have to admit the new reader resembles the old one in every particular. It slips just as easily into its mock croc sleeve, and it utters the same soft whoosh when I switch it on. On closer inspection, I can't make out any of the little scratches and slight dents that the old one had as a consequence of my hitting it when texts I had to read roused me to fury. But I know they'll come.

I put it to the test of the walk around town, trying to find fault with it so as to prove the fat man wrong, but it passes. The new reader works.

I get to the end of my typescript, reading it in the park and then the café, where I drink a tasteless beer I don't really want. How many copies can we sell of such a marvellous book? When all is said and done, that's been the question of my life. It is utterly comical to think that after all these years I still don't have the faintest idea what the answer is. I am a comical fellow.

It occurs to me that Adèle will be happy to have the new reader. She'll be able to watch the same soap as before, but with better definition. I hand it over to her when I get home and would gladly rehearse the sales patter, but Adèle doesn't pay as much attention as I had expected.

*

"I could hardly wait for you to get home. I've an odd feeling that my arms have shrunk this evening. You'll have to ease my back for me and rub in the pain-relief cream."

32

At Sabine and Meunier's wedding reception Valentine is wearing a flouncy white dress, and we dance rock & roll. She laughs, showing teeth that match her dress. We take a few gymnastic turns and I reckon the other guests must think I've recovered completely. There's a big crowd and if it weren't for the fact that everyone is wearing fancy dress you might think it was a marketing gala.

Meunier has chosen a very peculiar venue. It's an art gallery near Bastille called Maison Rouge, a cavernous L-shaped space with an aquarium-like object in the middle. It contains a black marble tomb set on a gravel ground. Presumably some artist has buried a few of his illusions in it, to induce feelings of joy and merriment.

"I had no idea."

"They make such a lovely couple!"

Valentine wants to dance some more and she'd be glad to carry on until I'm out of breath. Luckily for her, I've still got enough craziness inside me to provide her with a few more whirls.

*

"You're a good dancer," she says. "I would never have thought."

"The inner me is a heavy metal fan and my life has been one long rock around the clock. I'm a disco star in publisher's clothing."

"You should ask Maud to dance," she says.

"Ask her yourself."

"The two of us will tango later on."

A waitress puts a bonzai asparagus canapé under my nose and I eat it. A waiter puts a glass of champagne under my nose and I drink it. A second one comes and I drink that too. A third one comes. I usually have a rather strained relationship with champagne, but tonight it's slipping down. Sabine comes up and pinches my cheek, laughing at her own joke. I am sorely tempted to smack her bottom, but I reckon that would be out of order. After all, she is the bride—as her complicated get-up confirms.

Geneviève is wearing a flamboyant trouser suit and with Sam at her side works the room to reassure everybody that she really is here. Balmer has put on a tie to have the pleasure of wearing it unknotted. It's getting warmer. Snaps are taken with the tomb in the background and glasses in hand.

Meunier emerges nearby and out of concern for my well-being hails a young waitress so as to give her an order:

"Get something to drink for my friend Gaston!"

The party has come to resemble an ocean, the swell rising and falling and rolling towards me and pushing me along. I

yield to the tide with a feeling of great repose and indifference. Only when I find myself outside on the pavement with my glass still in my hand do I feel as if I have made some kind of mistake.

33

Outside in Boulevard Bourdon, the temperature is only 13°
centigrade. It's the canal that keeps the area cool. Ripples
make barges creak and groan at their moorings. I walk back
up towards Place de la Bastille with my glass in my hand. I'll
be able to raise a toast to the splendours of the city and to the
glory of spiders who spin their pretty webs so decoratively.
I hold my glass like a bunch of flowers, passers-by smile at
me and I acknowledge their smiles with a courteous nod of
my head. Bubbly!

I clink glasses with watermen in the Arsenal dock, I toast
the singers at the Opéra-Bastille, the *Colonne de Juillet* in the
centre of the square, the April sky above it…

I'm in front of a heated outdoor *terrasse* and the waiter
calls out to me.

"Sit down, and I'll give you a refill!"

The idea seems appealing. Nice waiter.

"Chablis, please. No bubbles."
    "Consider it done."

*

So I'm taking tiny sips of chablis to make the moment last. My legs are like jelly and I doubt I'll be able to stand up for a while. Passers-by go past like two-dimensional cut-outs, all at the same time, there must be thousands of them. The orange glow of the cresset above and behind me doesn't alter the fine golden-green hue of my chablis. I look through it to see the world in different shape and colour. I feel well. I'd like to have a manuscript to read. The waiter comes back with his excellent bottle.

"So that's where you are! You also managed to avoid the trap."

It's Balmer, in a slightly scruffier state, floating but not yet drowning. The end of his rolled-up tie droops out of his jacket pocket and his shirt is out of his trousers. He flops into a seat next to mine.

"Same for me, waiter! You see, Robert, I started thinking during the wedding ceremony, I'm going to do love stories only from now on. To be honest I think you can do anything with love stories: write history, talk politics, even do formal experiments. My last book is weak on feeling, weak on sex, weak on lust, it's too intellectual. Look at the girl Maud, I hate to say this, but with ten-penny-worth of feeling you can make 100,000."

"200,000."

"I have to get closer to my women readers. Same again, waiter, thank you. I have to work out a new form of romance

and its discontents. Invent new formulas: seduction, jealousy. Something like, there's this guy, and he meets a girl… Whoops! I must be off. Always overloaded with stuff to do. Say hallo to Adèle for me, I must fly, and also I'm really glad you approve…"

And off he slips into the evening.

34

The day Adèle died after a long and painful illness was quite beautiful. Cancer in the PR department pays little heed to the weather forecast. The sun shone brightly on Montparnasse, birds sang, flowers bloomed and trees treed. Even nearby Rue Froidevaux, with all that frozen meat in its name, couldn't chill the air.

I did not like the technical part of her death—dressing the corpse, families, hand shakes, kisses that went sloppy with tears, unrestrained hugging and so forth. Lame quips about the coffin they carried her off in made me smile, but not for long. I didn't much like Montparnasse Cemetery either: it's full already and you have to walk on other people's graves to get to your own.

The mourners included most of the folk who were at Sabine's wedding, together with the entire sisterhood of book publicists and a chunk of the firm she worked for. The whole crowd trampled on graves or tried to squeeze together on the narrow pathways. It was touching to see them huddle together. It was the spitting image of a Sempé cartoon.

My dear departed was settled into her grave and people paraded past. Two hired guys with strong arms put the

stone in place and then the crowd dispersed. End of the Sempé cartoon.

Then when it was all over and I was on my own, I was in a position to take advantage of the wonderful late afternoon sunshine. I turned down people who asked me out, I herded the stragglers and pushed them out of gates, then did a tour of the graveyard to pay respects to some of my friends. I'm not a great cemetery visitor, but I remembered where some of the plots were to be found. In fact, I never come here, but I answer when opportunity knocks. A few clumps of witch grass were growing between the graves, and some blue flowers peeped out at me from here and there. The air was transparent, the city rumbled on in the distance, widows in black were carting flowers around. A gardener trundled a tumbrel down the path.

A lady dabbed her nose as she asked me nicely if I had lost someone too. I was able to reassure her on that point. I must have dawdled for a while because dusk crept up on me. It was my turn to be herded out by the gardener with his front wheel advancing menacingly on my heels.

Once I'd got past the cemetery's long black wall, the city was lit up in its usual way. Car engines purred at the lights, Métro exits disgorged Zaziemen. I turned left down Rue de la Gaîté, thinking I might find a place to eat, but I decided to go home and have a meal by myself.

35

The brilliant weather hasn't wavered ever since. In my sun-drenched apartment I'm going round in circles like a lighthouse beacon.

I've stopped going into the office. To be precise, I've stopped altogether. Nothing doing. No up, no down, not for better, not for worse. Not going on, not going back. I'm standing, like an obelisk, but only faintly.

Adèle's death hasn't weighed on me very heavily, I don't really feel bereft, I got a lot out of her, I don't reach out for her mechanically, I know she's not around any more. I don't fumble for her in bed, I don't weep for her and I don't complain about her not being there. I don't harp on our being mere specks of dust. No, I'm alive, that's all, and I want to read.

It took two phone calls to transfer all my shares in Robswood to the youngsters and Balmer. At the end of the day I was the traveller they'd been waiting to rob on the electronic highway. Balmer told me I was crazy, that I was over-reacting to grief, that the start-up had a lot of value, that Monkey might not get to be a billionaire but could easily be a very respectable millionaire in jeans and a floppy sweater,

that I should think twice, and I told him I really didn't have any more time for all that. I had reading to do.

I went to my favourite bookshop. I hung around for a while with my hands behind my back, wandering along the shelves and between the display tables. For such a long while that conscientious sales-girls came up to me more than once to ask if I needed any help. I did not require any help. I was helping myself.

"I would like a box, please. You know, one of those cardboard boxes you use for returns."

"Right away, sir."

"How many books do you usually get into it?"

"Fifty or so."

So I set the bar at fifty. I could just as well have said ten or a thousand, but I plumped for fifty. The fifty books that my job has prevented me from reading and which I am now at long last going to read.

From Aragon to Fritz Zorn I make a methodical selection of titles and place them in the box. First editions, paperbacks, translations, major houses, small houses. I select some books to surprise myself, others because they don't really appeal to me, others because I've always been daunted by them. I shall read them, as you always do read books, with anger. I shall be free to be angry.

Why, when I get to the cash desk, does it occur to me that books are expensive? I've spent my whole life proving the opposite.

*

"Excuse me, sir, aren't you Robert Dubois, the former publisher?"

36

Books are now piled up on my desk like the wall of a castle. The box they'll go back into when they've been read is on the wood floor. At long last I'm behind a great battlement of print. Every day I used to think: "You have to read that" "If I had the time I would read this" "To think I still haven't read that" "Lucky are those who can read at their leisure" "If only I'd read this, I'd be a much better reader"…

Now here they all are in front of me. *Belle du Seigneur*, Rabelais' *Tiers Livre*, *Bonfire of the Vanities*, *Bardane par exemple*, Mallarmé, Roubaud, Féval's *Habits noirs*, *Around the Day in Eighty Worlds*, and Papillon's nonsense poems *en langage enfançon*. Their collective dimensions are exactly those of the field of silence stretching as far as I can see. I'm not in any hurry and I'm entirely stress-free. I know we're going to fight to the death. Reading will be a bloody business. They'll give me no quarter and I'll not let them get away with a thing. If necessary they will overwhelm me and I'll throw them at the wall in fury.

The refrigerator is fully stocked and the main door is locked. I've taken care to switch off the telephone, the television, sex and everything else.

It's a fine day and I don't give a damn. It's raining, and that's great. Blow, winds, and crack your cheeks.

I lay my reader and my mobile phone on the desk. I draft a last text to Valentine of the white dress: "Carry On Dancing". I sit staring at the devices for an interminably long time. I know they will slowly lose power and meaning. The day is waning and, after a long wait, I finally hear them writhing in pain. They utter their little alert sounds, clamouring for sustenance, and after a last spasm and a mortal ding, each sinks into the darkness of an electronic grave.

From now on the anti-depression committee will have no path by which it can reach me. I am a book-man and a man-book. My great wall protects me. And I read so as to take it to pieces, slowly and calmly. I shall pick books randomly and without premeditation, so reading will arise of its own free will, and I know it will be the right order. If you leave them to roam free, books can hardly be wrong.

I open the first page in the first book, I break the first spine, I shove my nose into it to have a good sniff and off I go.

When I've finished reading the last word of the last sentence of the last book, I'll turn over the last page and decide for myself whether the life before me is really the one I would still want to have read.

AFTERWORD

The use of literary constraints by the Oulipo serves different purposes, depending on whether the constraint is newly invented or else the refurbishment of a long-forgotten fixed form devised by one it its many anticipatory plagiarists.

The first role of constraint is to act as a stimulus to literary creation. By setting bounds on the imagination, it paradoxically makes writers more aware of the range of their freedom. That is why constraint has been so productive of new works. Propelled by an extraneous requirement, text spurts forth in the here and now, and helps writers to tack in the face of internal headwinds that might otherwise drive them onto the rocks.

Secondly, constraints challenge the formal conventions that we've accepted by conscious or unconscious collective submission, or out of historical inertia. In that role it is a tool for questioning the relationship between form and meaning. It turns the "leaden weight of meaning" into a secondary concern, allowing writers to see how the chosen constraint pushes meaning around, thus giving it the opportunity of making itself anew.

Broadly speaking, Oulipians indulge in constraints in two ways.

On the one hand, they produce fairly lightweight demos to show the constraint's feasibility and to explore its playful potential. Those texts are the ones that are published in the pamphlets of the *Biblothèque oulipienne* or else read aloud at one of the many public venues where Oulipians are asked to perform. On the other hand, when a longer work is to be based on one or more constraints, it's obvious that their deployment has to engage with the work's deeper themes. The constraint then becomes an integral part of the work.

Many critics, beginning with Bernard Magné, have shown that the absence of the *e* (the letter's name is pronounced in French like English "err") in Georges Perec's *A Void* is also the absence of *eux* (also pronounced "err")—meaning "them", that's to say, Perec's parents, who died respectively in the defence of France and in a concentration camp. It's also clear that moves in the game of go and a reflection on the sonnet form underlie Jacques Roubaud's poetry collection, ε. It is equally clear that the graph that controls the organization of Roubaud's *Great Fire of London* is a precise and mathematical mirror of the meanderings of his memory... Not to mention the profound underpinnings of Perec's *Life A User's Manual*.

When I had the more modest task of creating the disorder of all the possible out-turns for the African heroes of my *Chamboula*, I had recourse to a binary tree structure that I allowed to proliferate. As is well known, only a rigid rule can

generate true disorder by freeing it from the unconscious order of the world.

As for my *Dear Reader*, it struck me that the subject implied a reflection on the future of reading. As I say in the book, it is probable that one of the possible forms of reading in the near future will be interactive: readers will enter into the body of the text and adapt it to their taste, abandoning marginal notes and coming closer to the work of an author.

That is why I decided to give my book (probably one of the last of its kind) a fixed form based on its character count, so that anyone entering it to change a single letter will destroy the entire project.

The composition is therefore shaped like a sestina, a poetic form invented in the twelfth century by the troubadour Arnaut Daniel. It has the same number of stanzas (6) each having the same number of lines (6), and it follows the same rotation of rhyme words. The words *read*, *cream*, *publisher*, *mistake*, *self* and *evening* recur at the line-ends in accordance with the spiral permutation of the sestina.

The lines are of fixed length. As they serve to narrate the fate of a mortal man, they undergo attrition (melting snowball): the first stanza contains lines of 7,500 signs (including spaces), the second contains lines of 6,500 signs (including spaces) and so on down to the sixth, which consists of lines of 2,500 signs (including spaces). The entire composition makes a poem of 180,000 signs (including spaces).

PF

These constraints apply equally to this translation. Epigraphs and chapter-headings are excluded from the count.

French requiring in general rather more words than English to express the same thing (and consequently a rather higher number of signs (including spaces)), this translation contains some material that the author was obliged to omit from the original. Other liberties taken with the text arise mainly from a respect for constraint.

DB

Pushkin Press

Pushkin Press was founded in 1997, and publishes novels, essays, memoirs, children's books—everything from timeless classics to the urgent and contemporary.

This book is part of the Pushkin Collection of paperbacks, designed to be as satisfying as possible to hold and to enjoy. It is typeset in Monotype Baskerville, based on the transitional English serif typeface designed in the mid-eighteenth century by John Baskerville. It was litho-printed on Munken Premium White Paper and notch-bound by the independently owned printer TJ International in Padstow, Cornwall. The cover, with French flaps, was printed on Colorplan Pristine White paper. The paper and cover board are both acid-free and Forest Stewardship Council (FSC) certified.

Pushkin Press publishes the best writing from around the world—great stories, beautifully produced, to be read and read again.

STEFAN ZWEIG · EDGAR ALLAN POE · ISAAC BABEL

TOMÁS GONZÁLEZ · ULRICH PLENZDORF · TEFFI

VELIBOR ČOLIĆ · LOUISE DE VILMORIN · MARCEL AYMÉ

ALEXANDER PUSHKIN · MAXIM BILLER · JULIEN GRACQ

BROTHERS GRIMM · HUGO VON HOFMANNSTHAL

GEORGE SAND · PHILIPPE BEAUSSANT · IVÁN REPILA

E.T.A. HOFFMANN · ALEXANDER LERNET-HOLENIA

YASUSHI INOUE · HENRY JAMES · FRIEDRICH TORBERG

ARTHUR SCHNITZLER · ANTOINE DE SAINT-EXUPÉRY

MACHI TAWARA · GAITO GAZDANOV · HERMANN HESSE

LOUIS COUPERUS · JAN JACOB SLAUERHOFF

PAUL MORAND · MARK TWAIN · PAUL FOURNEL

ANTAL SZERB · JONA OBERSKI · MEDARDO FRAILE

HÉCTOR ABAD · PETER HANDKE · ERNST WEISS

PENELOPE DELTA · RAYMOND RADIGUET · PETR KRÁL

ITALO SVEVO · RÉGIS DEBRAY · BRUNO SCHULZ